Red Henna Blues

by

Jaspal Kaur Singh

Finishing Line Press
Georgetown, Kentucky

Red Henna Blues

I dedicate this book to my grandmothers, Laaj Kaur and Bishan Kaur, mother Tej Kaur, father Prab Joth Singh, daughter Gitanjali Kaur Singh, son Gautam Mohan Singh, and my granddaughter Karina Singh Cho.

Publisher: Leah Huete de Maines
Editor: Christen Kincaid
Cover Painting: Uzma Ahmad
Cover background photo: Jane Milke
Author Photo: Kym Ghee
Cover Design: Elizabeth Maines McCleavy

Order online: www.finishinglinepress.com
also available on amazon.com

Author inquiries and mail orders:
Finishing Line Press
PO Box 1626
Georgetown, Kentucky 40324
USA

Contents

III. Qisse and Kahaniyan

IV. aromas and colors of home

V. Full Circle & Back

Historical Photos of the Singh and the Extended Family from Burma

Acknowledgments

1. migrations, diasporas, homes

Interconnected: You and I

You were there: when I needed a tiny helping hand. You recognized me from before, lifetimes ago, when we were playmates, helping each other cross streams, climbing Shan mountains, relishing Rangoon heat. In flavors of mangoes, papayas, rambutans and mangosteens. In swaying palms and bamboos of the tropics and in Punjabi fields. You sang and danced for the simple joy of a farmer's life—fecund and ever-present.

Come to Taunggyi

The small town of Taunggyi—which literally means big mountain—in the Shan States of Burma is ablaze with pink cherry blossoms adorning the mountains. The cherry and pine trees, stirred by fresh breeze blowing from the Greystone Mountain, whispers, and then getting excited, shouts the news from the Shan people to all the others in lower Burma, especially to those dwelling in the hot capital, Rangoon—*Taunggyi go la khe ba! Come to Taunggyi!* The Crag, the rocky mountain of Shan, is looking at the valley with a benign eye while *Taung Chun*, the sharp mountain with its *Phaya Taung* pagoda, looks away to the east. The lovers' lane, *Mee Chaa Lun*, calls to all youngsters with passion in their hearts and hope in their souls, escaping their parents' eagle eyes, to break taboos and steal kisses. This borderland separates the mountains from the town, which is verdant with tropical trees, bamboo, padauk, weeping fig, while mauve, pink, white, and yellow orchids cling between tree trunks and branches, as if finding a cozy place to rest.

I transplant these orchid plants from the cool shade of the mountains by gently prying them apart from the low hanging branches and, when I get home, placing them in coconut husks tied together with coir twines, then hanging them from the avocado tree branches and the eve of the tin roof over the wraparound wooden veranda of our home. I tend to these colorful transplants very carefully, fearful that they might not survive away from their home. Each morning, I wake up early to water them, careful not to drown them and then gently touch them with my fingertips, one by one. My paternal grandmother Laaj, who hails from Rawalpindi in Punjab, and who has a beautifully lined forehead, like dried rivers, scrunches her eyes, her white chunni slipping from her white-haired head, and scolds me for touching them: *the oil from your fingers will discolor them; they will lose their beauty, first from having them transplanted from the mountain, and now from you touching them with greedy and dirty fingers!* But luckily for me and my family, they always manage to survive, blooming brilliantly to brighten our tinroofed home in the Shan States.

Our house is built:
of cement and golden teakwood
the upper wooded floor slatted and crocheted
and the lower cemented level surrounded by interlaced
fenced veranda while its corrugated tin roof—becoming a musical
instrument during monsoon seasons—hangs low to mossy grounds: the song raindrops
lullabies for us to burrow in bed during dreamy Shan mornings or snuggle and fantasize in
homemade quilts during balmy tropical Burmese nights in the lands of greenghosts

Fig. 1. Photo of Taunggyi, Burma by the late U Chan of Taunggyi

1917: Grandmother Laaj's Burmese Odyssey in British India

Grandmother Laaj, as a thirteen-year-old bride from Punjab, you traveled to the far reaches of Burma. You passed through unknown lands and seas, with a seventeen-year-old groom who worked as a spare driver on his uncle's lorry, ferrying goods from India to Burma for the colonial masters. On your wedding day, he gave you a tiny Burmese ruby ring and you imagined a life full of light and color, so different from the poverty and dryness of Punjab where farmers, like your family, starved.

Fig. 2: Laaj Kaur, circa 1978, in New Delhi, India.

New Home, Old Prejudices

Grandmother Laaj, when I was seven years old, you told me about Grandfather Meher's promise to his family members from rural Punjab in British India that they:

would travel to Rangoon in Burma and live like other Anglicized Indians in bungalows with English gardens—

would be educated and civilized like the English—

would do trade and have bellyful to eat and dine on rich chicken curries like Indian colonial administrators—

He forgot or deliberately left out the poor and struggling Indian working class in Burma, the ones who did the menial labor, the ones who traded by taking little bundles of cloth or spices to Burma, the ones who worked as dishwashers or lorry drivers, as he and his uncle did, driving for days from India to Burma on dusty and stony roads taking loads of hardware or pulses, living at first in poor tenements and then in shoddy bamboo houses with no running water or electricity, then in houses built on stilts by the swamps, dirty water draining in the yards and streets, mosquitoes infested with imminent threat of malaria, the ethnocentrism of many Burmese who saw the *kula mai*, the black foreigners, as invaders and British bootlickers, who took their frustrations of the British colonial rulers on the wives and children of the dirty *kulas*, turning up their noses at the "Indian smell," and chased their sons from schools, pulling their turbans off, chanting, *kula mai! kula mai!*

No, you said Grandfather Meher forgot or misremembered his difficulties and pain in Burma, and so you, your sons, daughters, granddaughters—all your descendants—were to walk in his footsteps and feel the agony of alienation and dislocation which he must have felt for his uncle, his mother, and the generations that went before and were to come after him in colonial and postcolonial India and Burma.

Fig. 3: Meher Singh, Laaj Kaur's husband, and the author's paternal grandfather, circa 1950

Anand Karaj: Re-memory of Laaj' wedding to Meher

Buddho, Meher's mother, readies the simple farmhouse for the wedding ceremony. Marigold garlands threaded together hang on the *darwaza* of the house. Like a chaste nakedness in their redolent smells. Her wedding outfit, a red salwar kameez and colorfully embroidered phulkari chunni, along with the small ruby ring that Meher had given Laaj, completes the ensemble. As the sun filters through the wide-open windows, the house glows as if readying for the bridal night.

The whole village of Peeyan begins to glow, too, like fireflies at the wedding. They had set earthenware lamps outside the door of each house to commemorate the event. At the Gurudwara, the wedding ceremony takes just a short time, but to Laaj, her head bowed behind her veil, the time seems interminable. The priest voice sounds like a benediction, but it seems to float to her ears from so far away, the *tabla* drums beating an incomprehensible message. As they slowly walk around the Gurugranth sahib four time, a soft pink fabric around their necks tied together in a ceremonial knot, Laaj thinks with half anticipation and half trepidation of her life in the unknown and far-off Burma.

The langar of *dal, roti* and *gobi* is eaten slowly as if a pleasure to be remembered years later, but all Laaj could think of was Meher's fingers rolling a piece of roti around the *gobi* and placing it in her *thali*.

Reminiscence of Silver Bells

Meher barely remembers Laajwanti, Laaj Kaur now. She is from a Hindu family, but is now a Sikh, as she converted to his religion through the marriage ceremony. So, when he sees her for the first time on his wedding night, he marvels at her robust and clear-skinned face, with her long black hair almost to her knees. He smiles through his shyness and grasps hold of her *parandi* tied to her shiny black hair, and hears her whisper, "I made the *parandi* myself." Laaj had worked for long hours and days to complete her wedding arrangements. She sewed her wedding salwar kameez, embroider the phulkari chunnis, made her *parandis*, and knitted sweaters for herself and for Meher. She heard the Shan mountains could get bitterly cold. When Meher tentatively, but gently, takes the trembling Laaj in his arms, the tiny silver bells on her *parandi* jingles delightfully.

Crow on Mango Tree: Buddho's message

Meher, still hearing the jingle of silver bells in his ears, dreaming of Laaj in Burma with him, his *saathi*, his lifemate, comes out of the hut and sees Buddho, sitting in the tiny kitchen with a pot between her knees, fingers twined around a rope, churning the sour cream into white butter.

Her voice vibrates as she celebrates his return. "*Weh! Leh!* Drink some fresh lassi."

"Nothing tastes the same as this lassi, Bebe," says Meher, his dark brown eyes smiling, as he wipes the lassi from his small mustache with his strong and long fingers.

"In a few years' time, I want to take you back to Burma with me. I have a small house built in Mong Nai, not far from Taunggyi, where I am promised a partnership in uncle's fizzy drinks factory."

Buddho looks out at the fields whose yield is getting smaller and smaller every year. She sighs, "I look forward to the day, *puttar. Rab karey*, it comes fast."

A crow, flying above the mango tree, begins to caw.

marriage & alienation

At the Gurudwara where you were doing *seva* in the kitchen, Grandmother Laaj, Buddho had looked at you and had told your father that you were going to be the one to bring Meher back home from Burma to Punjab to her someday. Within a week, you left your home and travelled for long days and tiring nights to Burma with your new husband.

The mountains in Shan States where he took you were a blazing pink color and you said you got worried that they were on fire. That was your first glimpse of the cherry blossom covered lush mountains of Shan States. Meher took you to the small bamboo house he had built in a little village away from the cities.

Snorting pigs roamed under the house built on stilts. You couldn't sleep for a long time.

Chakwal, Punjab: Great-Grandmother Buddho's Ancestral Village

A tall thin figure, her loose black *salwar kameez* flapping against her legs. Her *chunni* fluttering behind her & a vulture circles above. She turns at the corner of the dry field, looks back at the twilight horizon: solitary dark cloud drifting aimlessly.

> *No sight of her son. He promised*
> *to return from Burma. Take her with him.*

The mongo fruits, hard and sour on the tree, dangle and sway.

Her cow, Lacchi, dead in the well.

The sky is cloudless, moonless, and starless.

Suddenly, a crow caws from the tallest branch of the mango tree, swinging to and fro, crying desolately, *"Kaa . . . Kaa."*

the cockaded *turla* turban

The jungles of Mong Nai in the Shan States of Burma are full of dacoits and orchids. Sometimes, Laaj goes with Meher to pick the orchid plants. The dacoits are mostly poor Shans and Karens farm workers who are suffering immensely under the British. They waylay rich merchants or Sawbwas, the Shan royalty, on their way to visit relatives or attend weddings and loot them at gunpoint. These dacoits roam near the *Hopong Yei Hwet*—the Hopong Springs. Sometimes, they target poor traders as well.

Meher often travels on horseback through the thick jungles to reach Taunggyi. Before he married Laaj in India and brought her back with him to Burma, he had bought the horse Moti at one of the farm fairs in Taunggyi. "One day," Meher thinks, "I will let Laaj ride it. I will teach her well."

One night, as Meher returns from Taunggyi after a trading trip, he hears the cicadas thrumming and feels the darkness enveloping him and Moti. The cockaded turla on his turban ruffles in the cool mountain breeze. Suddenly, from the corner of his eyes, he sees two figures detaching from the darkness, commanding him to stop. "Dacoits," he thinks, and takes off at a speed, as his heart gallops along with Moti, all the while holding his umbrella like a rifle. He hears one of them say, "*Tannat shi dai, tadi hta!*" "Careful, he's got a gun!" Feeling the bittersweet taste of his heart in his mouth, he thinks only of escape and rides the tired Moti hard. Bending his head low, holding his umbrella high, his cockaded *turla* turban bouncing back and forth on his head, he hears gunshots, but rides on recklessly and determinedly. And: He escapes death due to his reckless but brave action—this time.

That night, after a warm bath in the outdoor *ghusalkhana*, and after eating some warm *roti*, *urad dal* and curd, he sits down on his stringed cot with Laaj, his long hair loose, while she, sitting next to him, gently massages his legs. His muscles are so strong, thinks Laaj, but he does look a bit agitated, as if his flesh, extra taut, might be strumming a *suneha*, a message. Softly, so as not to make a big deal out of another ordinary event in his Burma life, he tells her about the incident with the dacoits, laughing about the use of his umbrella. "Wasn't that clever? I made *ullus* out of them!" His laugh is like the dancing waves of the Daggar river in Chakwal. As his voice sinks in, she jumps out of the bed, crying, "*Hai Hai*, what if something happens to you!" He holds her in his arms, her face buried in his shoulders. "Laaj, Laajo, *bas kar*. I am safe now and I will be careful." He pulls her back to the cot, catches her long braid in his hand. She seems so vulnerable, even though her face, like the moon, is shining extra bright in the *diya* light. She turns to him, lifts her head from his chest, and whispers in his ears.

Next morning, Meher brings her a bag full of seasoned tamarind fruit.

1920: A son is born

At sixteen, Grandmother Laaj, you gave birth at home to my father, Joth, in Linkhe, a remote Shan Village. A Shan midwife assisting you, you drank caraway and anise infused tea which you prepared beforehand. The day before his birth, you went with Meher to the Hopong springs and swam in the cool waters—as a girl and not yet a mother.

You told me that when you were a young bride in Burma, you were fond of the *Nat Pwes* and would ask certain *Nats* for help with divining your fate.

Nats, spirits of young and beautiful people, often siblings who met violent deaths and became spirits, are worshipped by many communities in Burma. It was King Anawrahta (1044-1081) who first unified the various ethnic groups in Burma in the Irrawaddy delta and valley, recognized the *Nats* and brought them under the Theravada Buddhism umbrella. According to Buddhist understanding, these spirits, or greenghosts, unable to be reincarnated could possibly become dangerous, roaming the earth, lost for all eternity. It is believed that many of the rebels and rivals of the King Anawrahta met horrible deaths, but to appease the local polity, he incorporated them through ritual, declaring them guardian spirit of that region and installing their images in shrines. Most of the *Nat* rituals are conducted by *Nat Gadaws*, wives of *Nats*, who marry one of the *Nats* in a ritual and then becomes a medium for the spirit possession ceremonies. Many *Nat Gadaws* conduct ceremonies in the Shan States and many other parts of Burma at festivals, called *Nat Pwe*, or sometimes at private ceremonies.

Grandmother: Your father died in Punjab just before Joth was born. You visited a *Nat* ceremony. In the ritual, as the *Nat* spoke through a young virgin Shan girl, the sound of kettle drums reverberating on the Shan hills, you asked the spirit of your mother: Will you ever return to your home in Punjab and see your mother's face again?

Fig. 4: Laaj Kaur, in the center, along with the author's two paternal uncles, one on the right of the frame with sister, Bubbly, in her uncle's lap and one standing behind her. On the left of the frame is her neighbor and her children, circa 1944

1930: Dead Daughters

Your barely-crawling daughter died after swallowing quinine. Her name is lost. You came from a land where daughters are ritually murdered at birth even though in 1699 Sikh gurus prohibited the killings of female infants. You birthed three more sons and one more daughter, but she, too, died at fifteen from septicemia of the womb after giving birth to her own dead daughter.

Her name was Sundri, the beautiful one.

The boy whose long uncut hair got stuck in the mud

It is another sunny Sunday after a few rainy days in the village of Mong Nai. Laaj and Meher, after their children are born, moved from linkhe to Mong Nai to be closer to Taunggyi, the capital of Shan States. The traders and shopkeepers procured their merchandise at the Taunggyi five-day market at a competitive price. The bougainvillea bushes covering their bamboo home are aflame with red, purple, and white colored petals. The pink grapefruit tree is dangling with luscious golden skinned fruits. Laaj waits to wash her boys' long hair. But the boys have run away after breakfast. Suddenly, she hears them running towards her from the backyard, and as Joth and Shamsher run past her, she reaches out to grabs Joth's long braid. He screeches, less with pain and more with frustration. He hates cold water baths on Sunday mornings. *Weh, idhar aa!* Let me wash your hair! *Wekh, joowan naal parya siir!* She is so tired of taking out their lice and tics, for as soon as she gets them out, they go right back and swim in the filthy, muddy creek, run around with their long wet tangled hair with the other Shan village boys, and get the lice right back in them the very next day. Joth twists out of her grip and, before she could react, runs off at an incredible speed. Monkey!

It had rained a few days ago and the large creek is flooded. The few paddy fields around Mong Nai are submerged. Laaj, busy with kneading the dough to make rotis for their evening meal, is startled out of her revere about Meher who is off on one of his buying trips to Taunggyi when she hears Maung Maung shouting as he comes running to the hut. Breathless, he shouts that they can't find Ijotu, as the Shans call him. "He dove into the swollen creek quite a while back and has not resurfaced! Ko Ko and Min Thar dove after him, but they, too, have not resurfaced!" Maung Maung, along with Laaj, who overturned the copper bowl in which she is kneading the dough, runs to the creek. As they reach the ridge, breathless, they see him lying on the wet tall grass, his long hair all muddy and tangled, his friends laughing at the look on his face. It seems his long hair had got entangled to a big branch and then stuck to the bottom of the muddy water, and it had taken Ko Ko and Min Thar all their strengths to dislodge him from there. After she makes sure he is unhurt, Laaj grabs him by his hair and thrashes him within an inch of his life as tears run down her plump cheeks. His eyes red from the water, and his face flushed at the beating, he shouts, *"Ki ho gaya*! I am fine," and then suddenly laughing, he hugs her, lifts her up and attempts to swing her around. Another box to his ears, and he sobers up, knowing how worried Laaj must have been, especially as she is with child. He hugs her tight to his wet and skinny chest.

After washing his hair with her strong homemade soap, Laaj instructs Joth to sit in the sun to dry his hair. *Look at him scratch his head like a monkey!* As soon as it is dry, she intends to oil it with coconut oil and braid it into a long plait for him. He is still too young for a *joora*, she thinks, although in Peeyan you won't see such a strapping boy like him walking around in plaits.

Elsewhere

Laaj walks into the *rasoi,* sits on the *moora,* grabs some coal ash with the loose and wet coconut husks, and begins to scrub the dirty copper pot.

Soon, Joth, sitting in the sunshine and munching on raw green mangoes, is distracted by Ko Ko and Maung Maung, who are walking past their home with their *gwalay* catapults, and is away in a flash with them. Tying his hair in a sideway twist like the Shan people, he slings his Burmese bag filled with *lausas,* dried rounded mud pellets over his left shoulder, tests his *gwalay* by stretching the rubber, and away they go into the jungles to hunt birds and pigeons.

Joth returns home as the sun is setting, hungry and dusty from his day's antics, having caught only two sparrows and one pigeon, thinking of the curry Laaj would cook him with the birds, but also anticipating her wrath at being gone all afternoon, when he hears loud wails from across the lane from his uncle Arji's house. Heart pounding, he runs into the house. Laaj is wailing along with the women in the courtyard.

Munna uncle, Meher's cousin, when he was returning from Taunggyi after withdrawing some money from the bank, is dead, murdered. The money was for a new house he was constructing for his young family, and somehow, it seems the dacoits found out and ambushed him at the Hopong Yethwet jungle stretch. Some people had found his spare, the driver apprentice—the one who rides with Munna in his lorry—Achu, the Malayalee employee, who had barely escaped with his life, far from the murder scene. He is badly hurt. Another lorry driver, seeing the injured Achu, took him to a nurse near Taunggyi. Achu can be trusted with anyone's life, and particularly Munna's, as Munna had trained him since he was ten years old, his maid's son. Achu tells them that Munna had implored the dacoits to spare his life; *take everything, but please, leave me. I have small children.* As they took the money, and were walking away from them, Munna, the ever polite and well-mannered Sikh born in Punjab, asked, *May I go now, please?* They turned around mid-stride and hacked him to pieces right there; the grass around his body was flattened for yards as he struggled for his life. Munna was Joth's favorite uncle and Meher's best friend.

How could they do this to Munna uncle? Joth's emotions are confused and angry. He wants to get out of this godforsaken place and go elsewhere, where it will be safer.

Joth and May May: Laaj's *Qissa* of her son's letters

Joth still shoots birds and dives in the muddy creek that entangled his hair. He staggers home at night, tired from bird hunting, his hair disheveled and tied in a sideway braid. Laaj is tired of tying his hair in a *joora* early in the morning and seeing him later with it untied. She chides him for his unruly appearance, *devil's child,* she says, her dark almond shaped eyes crinkling, as she chuckles.

But he also plays the harmonium, opening and closing the bellow for the sweetest breath, to serenade the girls in the village. He learns the accordion, too, so he could walk around squeezing his desire for any girl to hear. But Joth wants only one person to hear his music— his favorite girl at school, May May, with her small flat nose and slanted eyes that he thinks are the most beautiful in the world. Most of the girls in village walk by the lane and pray for Joth's squeezebox to tickle their spines. He sings passionate Hindi songs accompanied by his instrument, the tallest and boldest of the boys, piercing their thoughts with his hawk nose and sexual eyes, and his voice seems to collect bits of laughter from the rushing brook.

May May feels his music, a petite girl with swinging hip-length hair—yes, her hair the color of dark rivers bedded down in moonlight. She looks for him each night outside her house, the fireflies as luminous as stars and the cicadas as melodious as Sufis in their songs. She sneaks out the back door to the bamboo grove, the moonlight filtering on to the soft grass, and grabs Joth's arms with both her hands, laughing and whispering: "IJoru. IJoru." Joth, his long braid wound around their warm bodies like a dragon, says, "May May, *chit tai naw* . . ." as they lie on the mossy ground bed in each other's arms, dreaming and whispering, unmindful of the fecund dew that impregnates them with desire as the night grows long.

In the morning, Laaj, suspicious of Joth's disappearance, sparks jocular remarks to her husband. Meher, aware that Joth's manhood seeds these long nights with a girl, decides his son must marry. When Joth traipses home shy and tired from sleeping in the grass, his father confronts him, knowing the consequences of Joth's actions. "You are only seventeen. Do you know the consequences of having a wife? Are you ready for the responsibility of marriage?"

For Joth, the moment to ask May May never arrives. As he gathers his courage to ask her to marry him, being fully aware of her father's disapproval, he receives news that she is engaged to be married to U Lwin, a schoolteacher from Mong Nai. He remembers U Lwin as a young, bespectacled and thin longyi-clad figure. . . Joth liked him as a teacher, and in his class he did very well, but U Lwin, the nerdy man with a sparse mustache?

Joth, agonizing at the thought of May May and U Lwin, as if a crocodile with a human in its belly, unable to eat or sleep for the next few days, waits in agony until the next full moon night. He rides by her teakwood house a number of times on his bicycle but doesn't catch a glimpse of her or her family. The house is set back from the road, surrounded by fruit and flower trees. They have often played badminton in that yard and sometimes they played *thauk see* with the neighbors' kids right there. But now the place appears desolate, and he hears only the bleak sound of his bicycle spokes in their revolution, as if cycles of lifetimes whirling by, and the forlorn cicadas, desperate for a glimpse of their mates, thrumming in vain—as he glides past her house.

The next full moon night, no clouds in the sky and birds hauntingly loud, Joth, eyes red with sleeplessness, long uncut hair rumpled, stands in May May's yard, near the bamboo grove. And his breath releases in slow motion as she rushes to him like he knew or hoped she would, like an arrow stretched to its limit, straight and sure, into his arms. After she hugs and kisses his face, alarmed by the worry in his eyes, she leads him to the mossy bank of a nearby brook. She spreads an old batik *longyi* on the grass and as they both lie down, she soothes his troubled face, slowly smoothing his lightly bearded cheeks, but the worry doesn't leave him.

"May May, how can you marry old U Lwin, the *ullu*?" Her round face never looked so beautiful as it does tonight, and he reaches out to entangle a hand in her long and lustrous black hair. She laughs at the Hindi term *ullu*, an owl.

"You knew my parents will never agree to our being together, IJoru, and neither will yours. You knew my brother had been snooping around my room, looking through my books for your letters. When I told him to get out, he slammed me against the wall. I am afraid for us."

The letters—every single one—and the word written by candlelight with such love, throb inside him. The thought that May May and the letters are being manhandled by her brother enrages him. He knows her brother well. He thinks he's better than anyone else in town. He works for the British administration and drives a jeep. She admits to Joth her brother has threatened to beat him up if he doesn't leave May May alone. Joth, unafraid of anyone or anything, considers May May's position and her fears. She hands him a bundles tied up with red strings, the letters.

Their bodies, like a tide, surge together, and he doesn't want to lose her. He'd rather drown in her limbs, smell her black hair in his hands one more time than live without her. The world is not yet ready for them, if it ever will be. She is from a Sawbwas family, a Royal Shan, while he is the son of a petty trader whose ancestors are from India.

The next evening, five tough Shan men enter Meher's shop and dismantle the bamboo verandah. Joth, doubled over from their blows, curses their fists. He falls to the floor but rises, taunting them. His shoulder, a battering ram, as he topples two of the men intent on destroying his father's hard work and business here. The others pin him against the wall, laughing; with blow after blow that bloodies their angry hands, they almost disfigure his face—but he glares at them fearlessly, the merchandise strewn on the dirty road.

May May marries U Lwin before the month of Natdaw's is upon Mongnai. Joth runs off to Taunggyi, vowing never to think of May May again. He enrolls himself at the American Baptist Missionary School.

1940: American Baptist Mission School

Grandmother, your son Joth, ran away from home at the age of seventeen. He came to the capital of Shan States, Taunggyi, Big Mountains, and enrolled himself in the American Baptist Mission School. Learning English and wearing long pants for the first time at the school, he tied a turban on his long un-cut hair (which he fashioned into a loose topknot). He felt like he was no longer a *junglee* who used to run barefoot in the Linkhe forests with his long sideway braid hanging down his shoulders almost to his bottom. You followed him to the city and opened a trading shop. Behind your shop was a country hooch shop where drunks used to stagger in and out all day long. You didn't mind as your shop faced the beautiful Sikh Temple.

Joth refused to worship at the Temple.

He taught you all to be modern.

Fig. 5: The author's father, Prab Joth Singh, circa 1935 in Taunggyi, Burma

Learning to tie a turban

In Taunggyi, the fashionable capital of the Shan States, Joth learns how to tie the turban—and his crooked sideways braids are behind him now. His brown face looks to an education as his body learns how to breathe the cool modish mountain air. Under the tutelage of a Mr. Brown, a small, mustachioed teacher from Manchester, England, whose bow tie neatly knotted represents efficiency and precision as much as England itself, teaches Joth English at a relative speed comparable to a boy learning how to ride a bicycle. Each time he falters in a sentence or tense, he must climb back up on that shiny bicycle and begin pedaling all over again.

Joth, who has never seen a white man before, embraces the correctness of language, the usual morning address, and even understands how his own father's drinking habits have no place in this empire of English and the most correct of phrases. Mr. Brown plays a phonograph record of a man singing Gilbert and Sullivan—and the fast, silly singing affects Joth in a strange way as he sees there's more to learning English than the ordinary addresses between teacher and student. For Joth, the schoolroom is part of the British Empire, or that part of his education.

A few years later, Joth, now almost twenty and a speaker of English, sports a small mustache and a goatee on his handsome face. Sometimes he hears the silly verses of Gilbert and Sullivan and can't restrain himself from humming a melody that some of the students found offensive in the classroom, but not Joth—he accepts the music for its eccentric lyrics and highly charged melodies as part of an Empire.

Picture him strolling down the Taunggyi Road. He spies a petite Sikh woman, long braided plait hanging down to her waist, walking by with another young girl, presumably her younger sister. Joth feels he has met his soulmate. Little does he know that she'll be the mother to his six children. That year, 1942, in the month of June, Tej, Joth's future bride, doesn't raise her eyes as she walks by him, making a beeline for the tailor's shop down the street. The tailor's shop, Undi's Tailors, run by Jai Singh, is located in a new building on the main road, owned by one Aziz with a pencil thin Clark Gable mustache.

Fig. 6: The author's father, Prab Joth Singh, circa 1942 in Taunggyi, Burma.

Home behind a shop

Most of the Indian people live on one side of Taunggyi's main road. That side of the town is flanked by Yat Daw Mu Phaya Mountains, with the tall standing Buddha to guard over it. There are also two Hindu Mandirs as well as two mosques on this side of the town. The Sikh Gurudwara stands on the other side of the main road. Across the road from the Gurudwara is the local bar. Within a month of Joth's leaving Mongnai, and the ever-growing threat of the Soabwas, Meher and Laaj decide to sell their small trading shop, their bamboo home, and move to Taunggyi.

Meher buys the shop next to the bar and they start a shadow life to the one Joth leads in Mr. Brown's classroom. Joth learns how to write English, seated at a desk, admiring the dips and curves of handwriting as if a woman's sensuous body. At the shop Meher sells almost anything, but not words. Joth tells Meher his family is lucky to not live above their shop. Then they'd be the Indians living above their father's shop, as most other do. Instead, they live behind it.

Transformation of Maya: magic or illusion?

My maternal grandmother, Maya Dei or Devi, as she was then called, when she was a little girl, used to live in a house in Bodh Wali Galli, the Bodhi tree lane, shaded so well that sometimes the sun seems to be blotted out from the day—not far from the well with the pump, Bambey Wala Khuh by the Elephant Gate, Hathi Darwarja in Amritsar, Punjab.

Every Sunday a parade of Maya Devi's family forms a line like ants, as they walk single file to the Harmandir Gurudwara. Asha Devi, her little sister, her parents, and her oldest brother, Gurdeep. She loves being with the family, and especially, her sister, who is also, like her, of marriageable age, and their conversation always turns to marriage.

At the Vasakhi da Mela, as Maya and Asha dressed, in their new yellow *salwar kameez* suits, laugh and giggle as they try on green and red glass bangles, their father looks at his wife sideways, and says, "It is time to make Maya's hands yellow. Ask Gurdeep to go and talk to Jai Singh's family." Mataji, the girls' mother, nods, looking at her carefree daughters, and sensing many males' eyes on them, and feeling the ancient fear of a mother of daughters swelling inside her, resolves to have the matter settled before the next full moon.

Gurdeep, a tailor like his father, sells his readymade kurtas and pajamas at one of the Harimandir *galiyans*' small shops. For Gurdeep, mornings begin with fresh goat milk, and after waking Bapuji with a cup of *cha*, he prepares breakfast for the whole family. Each day he worries about his sisters, who their husbands will be, their future stitched into the sewing he needles carefully—biting off the thread with his teeth: where will their fates take them? Next week, a prospective bridegroom's family from Walla Verka, a small village near Amritsar, is coming to talk to him about Maya, his sister, who is already sixteen years old. She should have been married off years ago.

Gurdeep consults his father about the prospective groom, Jai Singh, who has just returned from Burma after five years. Like them, he is also of tailoring caste, which should not matter, as the Sikh social reformers preach. Even though he is twenty-one and considerably older than Maya, he is from a respectable family and has made his name known in the community as an established tailor with his own shop in Burma. They all know that Jai, as a hardworking boy of just sixteen, had taken off to Burma with his uncle, learning the trade as an apprentice tailor who also washed dishes and did odd jobs for his uncle's family and only learned to sew small shirts and frocks late in the evening, after all the choses were done—just to learn and practice the trade.

Maya, who, at sixteen, realizes that the time has now come for her to marry and go to live with her future husband in far-off Burma, worries day and night about the distance, and about Jai Singh, who at twenty-one, appears so mature and well-traveled. Her sister tries to persuade her not to go to Burma, having heard about all the man-eating Shans, Nagas and Manipuris, and advises Maya not to marry him. But Maya knows she must. Bapuji has so many worries. His tailoring shop is not doing so well, as there is so much competition in the small area they live in near the Golden Temple. Maya knows it is time.

Gurdeep sews her red salwar kameez, her wedding dress, and her sister and Mataji prepare the red *chunni* with gold trims. Maya herself created the *mukaish* dotted embroidery by pressing and knotting tiny silver threads into the chunni. Her sister though tries to persuade her to postpone the wedding for a year or at least stay back for a year after the ceremony. "I will never see you again," her voice echoes, as if coming from within a deep well, and Maya doesn't realize her prophecy will come true—she won't ever return as a young girl or woman, only when she's extremely old, but she doesn't know it then.

Maya, her deep almond-shaped hazel eyes narrowed against the Amritsari morning sun on the way to the Gurudwara, thinks deep and hard. If she doesn't get married, her sister will also remain a burden to Bapuji. Gurdeep has been holding off his marriage to Sajjo, their uncle's daughter, as he hopes to have his sisters wedded before he brings his bride home to their small, two room home. Maybe she will ask Bapuji to postpone her *doli*, the sending away ceremony, for one year?

After the short and simple *Anand Karaj* ceremony, where the priests first recite the *gurubani*, and then sing *kirtans* at the Harimandir Sahib, as Maya and Jai circumambulate four times around the holy book, she is renamed Bishan Kaur. She had still carried her traditional name of Maya Devi to this day, and even though times are changing in Punjab, her family had resisted the change. Sikh girls must now use their last name as Kaur, meaning princess, and not Devi anymore to distinguish the Sikhs from the Hindus. Male Sikhs had been named Singh, the lion, by the last Sikh Guru, Gobind Singh in 1699. It was to erase caste markers and to create the Khalsa, the saint soldier, as the baptized Sikhs came to be known. Maya feels transformed, as if her name change to Bishan Kaur is the casting off of old skin like a cobra— spiritual and godlike.

The bridal party returns to Maya's after the *langar*, the communal meal in the temple the house is no longer her home. The family prepares for the *doli* ceremony when the bride will be sent off to the groom's home. As the ceremony is about to begin, her face covered with the *ghunghat* of her red chunni, the *mukaish* creating a chiaroscuro of light reflections and shades of dark on her cheeks and eyes, illuminating a prismatic future full of potential, Maya decides there and then to go to Burma right away, after all.

Jai: dishwasher and tailor's apprentice

When Jai, my maternal grandfather, as a sixteen-year-old had first decided to go to Burma, his father, who was struggling to feed his family as a poor tailor, said, "*Na chal Burma nu, tere lekh jaangey naal.*" Don't go to Burma, your fate will follow you there. When he travelled from Amritsar to Calcutta and then on to Rangoon with his distant uncle, he had been incredibly lonely and scared, first time in a train and then a ship, waves as big as the top of the golden temple spires, but when they arrived in Taunggyi, the small Sikh community quickly made him feel at home.

He was an apprentice tailor at his uncle's shop, learning to hem and sew buttonholes, and washed their dishes and clothes for his keep. He worked extra hard, hearing his father's words—your fate will follow you—in his dreams, but five years later, he opened a little tailoring shop on the Taunggyi's Main Road. It took him many years before he returned to Punjab to marry at his father's continued behest.

Jai, happy now that Bishan is ready to accompany him to the Shan States right after the ceremony, thinks proudly of introducing her to his family in the village. After one month in the village of Walla Verka with his new bride, Sherney, city girl, as he begins calling her, Jai and Bishan board a train at the Amritsar station for Calcutta. Bishan, disoriented from travelling for five days from Amritsar in the train, becomes severely sick in the ship to Rangoon. The constant sound of the train tracks pounds in her head and the rolling of the ship in the ocean has her nauseated for days even after they arrive in Rangoon. They stay at the Rangoon Sikh Temple for almost a month before Bishan is ready to travel to Taunggyi in the mountains of Shan States. Jai, who is more seasoned in his travels by now, is extremely gentle with his little city girl.

In Taunggyi, the capital of Shan States, where many Punjabis have settled, the Indian community welcomes Bishan Kaur in their midst. Before leaving for India, Jai had stocked up his shop with *khaddar*, cotton, and some English poplin. She would survive in the back quarters, his young, dark-haired , soft skinned wife who doesn't know much about cooking or sewing. Jai takes to cooking meals in the mornings, so that Bishan wouldn't get overwhelmed in her new home.

Bishan, with her husband's help, buys the needed groceries from the five-day market. She finds a place for every item in the cupboards, arranging everything neatly. She resists daily to walk into the shop and visit her husband, for she finds his handiwork fascinating, as she fears it will distract his customers. His sewing, the stitches like little steps leading to the other side of fabric, has an artist's touch, and his reputation continues to grow. He makes enough to feed his little wife and himself lavishly, and they are happy. Bishan makes sure to keep her cupboards full. He continues to cook for them in the mornings. She admires his sewing and wishes she could be one of the stitches he encloses in a fancy dress with beads. She would hold her place there forever.

Coconut Chicken Noodles

Saya Sein, a local schoolteacher, visits the tailor shop frequently and considers Jai his close friend. He sits and chats with Jai for hours, talking about the British as their mutual enemy and wondering if someday they would become a free country. Their voices drift out from the back of the shop, meeting the heat outside with their own heated words. Saya believes they will never be a country without those who want to enslave them. Jai understands, and worries, and thinks about Punjab and India and considers the difficulties they're already facing. Sometimes, Saya invites them over to his place and cooks them Shan food. He serves the company salted green tea, coconut chicken noodles and hand-mixed papaya salad, and hears Jai's heated words simmer, then disappear after an authentic Shan dinner. Saya Sein gives Bishan the coconut chicken noodles recipe.

In all the decades she will live in Burma, Bishan will only learn one Burmese dish—coconut chicken noodles, which she will pass on, decades later, to her own daughters.

II. Traumas and Alienations: Love Stories

her stories

Bishan learns to knit, as she sees all the young wives creating beautifully patterned shawls, sweaters, baby clothes, and especially those cute little booties. Most evenings, she waits for her husband to accompany her towards forest quarters for a walk. She walks by his side, so close to each other, seemingly stitched together, as the famous tailor and his beautiful wife. They sit on one of the banks of the three lakes for a short time, and Jai, listening to her Amritsari Punjabi, the style of re-telling famous Punjabi *Qisse*, the ancient love tragedies, of Heer and Ranjha, Sohni and Mahival, and other folk tales realizes how mesmerized he is with her being. Her poetic rendering of the couplets and *slokas* of the Gurugranth Sahib has him so thankful for the good fortune of having found her in the busy city of Amritsar.

One evening, as they leave the cool shadows by the lake, she tells him she is pregnant.

An Anglophile is made, not born

Bishan and Jai's firstborn adds to their happiness. The local midwife, *Sayama* Beauty, delivers her eight-pound boy to her breast in the backroom of the shop.

"He is going to break hearts," *Sayama* says of this first child, named Amar, the eternal one.

Jai's tailoring work increases, so he begins stocking bits and pieces of imported fabric from England, as well as Indian weaves, but mostly, he buys handwoven fabric and cloth from the Inlay Lake area.

When Amar turns five, Jai walks his son to the Convent School, willing to trust him to the nuns' world of Christian religion and modern English words. On his way there to the school, Jai imagines him as a man who works along with the English in the British Administration. At the threshold of the convent school, with its haunting smells of soap and incense, Jai hears a nun leading her classroom in English sentences. Like a warbling bird, her voice soars above the others. He looks down upon his son with his trusting brown eyes, hoping this school will make a sahib out of him.

Every classroom uses English as their guide to education. Amar, their first child, bears the burden of having to be the best—and learning how to speak English and be like the English.

Convent Girls

Grandmother Bishan Kaur, Sherney, looks up from cooking a stuffed bitter gourd, and asks her oldest daughter, Tej, to knead the *atta* for *rotis*. Tej, washing her hands and drying them on her muslin *chunni*, walks to the corner of the kitchen and lifts the lid of the copper bin for freshly ground wheat flour. Tej's little sisters, Meeto and Bansi, enter the tailor shop and Jai Singh lightly taps the young girls' uncovered heads. He likes them in their Convent School uniform, which he himself had sewn. He walks with them to the back rooms where they live behind the shop.

To Tej, the smells of bitter gourd are like the days her sisters spend at the convent school, learning English words from the nuns which they repeat to her sometimes, but she is told she's too old, at twelve, to go to school anymore. Meeto walks to the bedroom and empties the contents of the school bag on her bed: a book of English poems, a ruler and a pencil. Tej can hear the strict marching of the verses in their meter—the nun teaching her sisters their language, as she lifts her arm up and down, as though the words continue down a dusty road to glory.

Tej looks up from kneading the dough, a faint hint of envy in her eyes. Her brothers and sisters can read English poems about strange places like Dover Beach and find some sort of meaning in the words, while Tej has only been to the Gurudwara Sikh school where the Gurmukhi language is taught only up to the sixth grade, and after she could read the Gurugranth Sahib and was introduced to the music of it, Bapuji removed her from the school. She must help Bishan take care of the baby, Kaka. Her mother, after the last birth became weaker, and lying on her bed, she sometimes speaks about her sister and about the Golden Temple in Amritsar, humming, "*Ram, Ram karta sub jug phirey . . .*" Tej croons to little Kaka. She sews him a velvet kurta with little pearl buttons. She rocks him to sleep, while Bishan rests her tired body, her genteel Amritsari mother.

Her brother Amar returns home with stories about the long sleeves of nuns concealing rulers, books, and cigarettes. They are rapped over the knuckles with the wooden ruler for being loud in class or daydreaming. But they too know "Dover Beach" as well as *Paradise Lost*, and are surprised that the nuns talk so freely about the free will of Satan.

Tej asks endless questions. She doesn't know if any of their answers are truth or fiction. Amar brings home wrinkled copies of the latest Punjabi magazine, *Preet Ladi*, some journals, and novels by Amrita Pritam, and tattered editions of Punjabi newspapers for the hungry Tej. Amrita Pritam's poems, published in *Amrit Lehra, Immortal Waves*, when she was just sixteen, are so different, so . . . what is the word? vibrant and bold, as compared to her life in Taunggyi. Tej yearns to write like Amrita, maybe not as a poet, but as a short story writer?

But cooking comes first. She takes the *datri*, the curved knife nailed to a wooden block, sets it between her feet, then placing the tomato between her fingers, glides it efficiently and quickly across the sharp edge of the knife. After this, she takes some green chilies, freshly washed coriander leaves, an onion, and cut them all in equally small parts and place them into an enamel bowl. Finally, she grabs a lime, cuts and squeezes its green heart over the sliced vegetables, sprinkles salt and pepper over the mixture. The salad is ready. She rolls the rotis, placing them on the iron skillet, and sees them turn golden. She looks up to see her sister coming into the kitchen to help with dinner. She collects the half-cooked rotis, slip them between iron tongs and lays them on the red embers to puff. Afterwards, she smears ghee on them and slip them between the cotton cloth, the one she embroidered with colorful threads, an English garden, to keep warm. She hands them to Meeto and Bansi.

Bishan Singh smiles at his daughters—a smile that spreads from ear to ear and rounds his bearded mouth. He ceremonially lays the rotis on the kitchen table. As he arranges the enamel plates on the wooden table, he looks at his wife who looks weak and tired. Weak after Kaka's birth, her resistance to colds have been low. He could feel the low vibrations of her breath in his bones, the notes trembling and deepening every day. His smile fading, he becomes pensive and meditative.

He remembers when he first married her, a young girl determined to live a good life. Her name then was Maya: magic or illusion? His daughters stare at him frozen by the table—his brown face like a salad of many parts, the eyes straining for something in the past, his mouth speaking words to someone, and his eyebrows in their bushiness crowded with other evenings. He has stepped somewhere else for a moment, perhaps to *Bodh Wali Gali* in Amritsar, and they never know when he comes back if he is ever the same.

Fig. 7: The author's mother, Tej Kaur, circa 1938 in Taunggyi, Burma

A crow walking like a swan

In high school, Amar starts staying out late at night. His friends, rich and cynical children of the Indian and Burmese business community, behave like Englishmen. It is the language they use, what guides them badly, urges them to behave a certain way. Bishan, worried, understands everything for when the crow starts walking like a swan, no good comes of it. The nuns think highly of him, however, and even if they don't know, they still might suspect that he drinks liquor with his friends. Jai suspects it—maybe because he thinks like a nun, always willing to investigate further into a certain situation, asking around, surmising, coming to a conclusion.

But they can do nothing, as Amar, now in high school, speaking fluent English and reciting Byron's poetry at co-ed gathering, is popular with the monied class and is invited to all their big homes—so, like the crow who thinks it is a swan, he continues to glide along Taunggyi streets in his polished black leather shoes.

When Amar finishes his matric, he gets a job with the British administration. He starts as a clerk and now has a steady income. Bishan is so proud of her son—so tall and broad shouldered, with well-cut trousers and a crisp, starched shirt, and Gandhi style glasses for his armor. His striped tie hangs around his neck, a silken reminder where he has to go and fight for his place in an English world.

Breakfast before the Convent

Breakfast of paronthas and eggs, and conversation with mouthfuls, a panic in the air, hands hurrying the last bits of food so they can reach the convent in time for morning mass. Meeto and Bansi look smart in their convent school uniform. Bishan makes sure their hair is tidy and their ribbons ironed. It is Amar who had fought to have his two younger sisters enrolled in the English school. As Tej was deemed too old to continue to study, she learns to read English from books borrowed from her sisters.

Knowing that Tej likes to read Punjabi books, Amar makes sure to give her all the old copies. She must learn to be progressive, like Gurbaksh and Amrita.

Sometimes, he lets her borrow his copy of Byron's poems, as Tej has taught herself to read English from her sisters' English school books.

One day, Amar hears Tej reciting Byron:

> There is a pleasure in the pathless woods,
> There is a rapture on the lonely shore,
> There is society, where none intrudes,
> By the deep sea, and music in its roar:
> I love not man the less, but Nature more.

A Utopia: Preet Nagar

At tea with Dara, his close friend, Amar, thinking of his traditional Sikh family, says, "Gurubaksh is radical and writes about love. He says that love transcends the caste system. People who love each other must marry whom they love, irrespective of their caste."

Dara looks at him, assessing his words, especially "irrespective of their caste," as if what he has said lashes his neck.

Amar knows that look. It weighs down Dara's face and makes it stretch. "I agree," Dara suddenly says. "Why do people believe in all these archaic notions of caste anyway. Thank God, Sikhism does not believe in it."

Amar laughs, preparing more lashes for his friend: "Are you serious? Haven't you noticed how the Sikh community segregates itself along caste lines? Don't you remember what a fuss the Chopras created when their son decided to marry that Jat Hindu woman?"

Dara studies Amar's face and nods. "You are right, they did. But that is only one case. Most of the time, however, they don't care about caste as the Hindus do."

"Remember," says Amar, "how the Mehta's boy was punished when he fell in love with a poor Burmese woman? It was not even to do with caste then."

Caste, class, race, creed, religion—if one is educated, do all these things matter? Amar doesn't think so.

Amar, who is in love with Rosy, Dara's sister, knows that her family would never agree to them marrying, as he comes from a tailoring caste. Dara's family, coming from a merchant caste, is also rich and highly westernized. Rosy, already at a university in Rangoon, is in love with Amar. He remembers when she was with him, as they used to roam *Meechan Lun*, the Lovers' Lane, kissing and necking, and told him once, "Amar, my family will kill me if I marry into your family. You know that. So, stop being so romantic. Life must go on for us without each other, even if it breaks our hearts." Was she really serious though? Will their love not survive in the face of family opposition?

He doesn't have long to wait to get his answer. Next year, Rosy marries Harry, the son of the Rangoon Singhs, who has a car dealership, one of the biggest in Burma. Everyone says the couple, a perfect match, seems so in love.

Two years later, Amar, as if coming out of a dark fog, forces his friends, the gang of six who used to hang out with him and Rosy, one of whom is her cousin, to arrange his marriage with Bachan Kaur of Shwenyaung, a little town near Taunggyi. They had told him of her great beauty, skin so light as to look milky and cheeks so pink that they resembled roses. He knows he must forget Rosy and move on.

It is only after the Anand Karaj, when Amar sees Bachan Kaur's hennaed hands resting on her red chunni on her lap, hands so dark that the henna almost looked blue and purple, that he begins to panic. And it is only when they are alone in his room late in the evening, and he urgently lifts her *ghunghat*, the veil, from her bowed head, and sees a dark face with thick eyebrows, a button nose, that he realizes he has been misled by his so-called friends. He remembers how much Rosy's cousin used to hate to see them together, saying they were from different caste and class, but he never thought he and his other friends, all from the merchant caste, would betray him in such a way. How dare a tailor's son . . . ?

A few days later, after attempting to have a conversation with Bachan, he realizes that she is a simple village girl, uneducated and afraid to speak, but by then, it is too late. He does attempt to take her back to her family, begging them to understand how mismatched they are, but they refuse, saying, only her dead body should leave her new home. Jai, who had urged him not to rush into marriage with an unknown girl, now says definitively, "Marriage is for life."

Amar, who comes to love and hate Chindo, as he begins to call his wife, uneducated but hardworking and loving, drinks everyday after work, reading Byron, looking for his Preet Nagar, his utopia, and reciting, in his drunken baritone voice, Gurbaksh Singh's words and Preet Nagar's motto into the wee hours of the mornings:

> Kisey dil saanjhe di dhadkan,
> Kisey preet-geet di leh,
> Pattey preet-lari dy dassan,
> Jis vich proti sabho sheh.
> (The beat of a common heart,
> A melody of love,
> Is what the pages of Preet-Lari
> —a rosary of love—speak of.)

1943: magical laddoos

Grandmother, you and Meher sold tea bags, sugar, salt, homemade biscuits, and rough cotton cloth to the Burmese—Shans, Indas, Pa'Os, Indians, and Chinese—in a small tin shack on the main road of Taunggyi across from the Sikh Gurudwara. Your firstborn, Joth, at twenty-year-old, saw Tej, her long braid swinging behind her back, walking out of her father's tailoring shop from across the street, and his heart missing a beat, dreamed of her for many days and nights. He glimpsed her again at the gurudwara with her sisters, helping prepare the *langar* in the kitchen, so he volunteered to serve the congregation just to be near her. He saw Tej and her two younger sisters looking at him with curiosity, especially as Tej, looking sideways at him, would lift the corners of her lips in an endearing way, and they would all giggle softly together.

Months later, Joth begged you to ask Tej's hand in marriage for him. You were opposed to the match, as she came from a tailoring caste. You were proud of your merchant case. Also, her immigrant father, hailing from a village near the genteel city of Amritsar, refused the match, eying the louts, your sons, from the village. Since Joth was adamant, you agreed to approach Jai Singh, albeit reluctantly.

The magic of your *laddoos* and your honeyed Rawalpindi tongue bewitched Jai Singh, and his city wife, Sherney, Amritsari Bishan Kaur, for Tej and Joth were soon married in the small Taunggyi Gurudwara that year.

Fig. 8: The author's mother, Tej Kaur circa 1944 in Taunggyi, Burma

Fig. 9. The author's parents, Prab Joth Singh and Tej Kaur, circa 1944 in Taunggyi, Burma.

1944: A knotted promise

Burma was now occupied by the Japanese.

There were fifteen wedding guests at the Taunggyi Sikh Gurudwara temple, as Tej and Joth walked around the Gurugranth Sabib. Tej, dressed in a red salwar kameez sewn by Jai, her father, held on tight to the pink *palla* which was looped around Joth's young shoulders and placed in her henna red hands, binding them to each other for ever.

Shamsher, Joth's younger brother, became a coolie, carrying loads for the Japanese and Indian officers marching towards Delhi to take India back from the British. Joth was exempt, as he was married and had responsibilities. Joth never forgot his brother's sacrifice, who went in his stead as a Burma-born "son of India," as Netaji Subas Chandra Bose called them, when he came all the way to their hometown to beseech them to take India back from the British.

That year, Grandmother Laaj, your first grandchild, a girl, Bubbly, was born to Tej and Joth. Although your heart was sore for your missing son, and saddened at a girl born in the family, you still made *laddoos*, a ritual dedicated to the birth of sons and shared them with your family and friends. You prayed for a grandson the next time around, so you could walk tall among the Indian community with your head held high—like the rich KT Company women with their sons at the Sikh Gurudwara every Sunday.

1945: Occupied Burma

When the Allied Army rained bombs on Japanese occupied Burma, Grandmother, you, along with Tej, and your first granddaughter, a baby of one, hid in the jungles near the biggest lake in Southeast Asia, Inlay, where the fisher people lived in huts built on stilts on the water. In this place, the lake dwellers would move around from home to home in small canoes rowed by foot while standing. Joth carried two bags of salt from your shop to barter for food but, one day, Tej, as she was off to barter some food, had an accident, as her canoe overturned, pitching the one salt bag into the water. She couldn't swim and feeling sure she was dying, flayed around in the shallow water, shrieking for help. She was rescued by an Intha man who was fishing near the accident in his small boat. She lost her voice and her mind for a week, then, on the seventh day, she began railing against you, heaping curses, calling you a demanding and controlling mother-in-law.

With her brother, Amar, she then sat silent in the shade of the red banana trees in the Inlay Phaung Daw Oo Phaya Buddhist monastery, listening to pagoda bells and monks' chanting, suckling the infant in her arms. Tej finally regained her senses after two weeks when she began seeing the distinct ochre colors of the monks' habits and heard the chants

> Buddham saranam gacchami
> Dhammam saranam gacchami
> Sangham saranam gacchami

on their lips and returned to the hiding place.

Tej alone cooked for the family with scraps and food foraged in the jungle or bartered with the rest of the salt. When the cicadas thrummed, all the people hiding in the jungle came out to Joth's hut to listened to the VOC on the only radio in the Inlay Lake area in the darkness.

Legend has it that one night, as my parents laid in each other's arms, Tej saw a shooting star from the open window and wished for a son to redeem her respect in your eyes.

At this time, you didn't know Satya (meaning truth), your second granddaughter, would be born in Punjab and not in Burma, as the land would be ripped apart by the departing British. You would feel shame.

Fig. 10: The author's sister Bubbly in her paternal uncle's lap with his younger brother on the left of the frame with some friends in the fields of Taunggyi, circa 1944.

1946 British India: Will you be Indian?

Pregnant and exhausted, Tej followed you, Grandmother Laaj, and the rest of the family to the train station, leaving all that she remembered and loved behind: her siblings and parents, her beloved birthplace, Taunggyi, Burma, for your childhood home in Rawalpindi in Punjab, British India. The Japanese occupation and the Allied Army's bombing and hiding in jungles had finally exhausted your spirits and your husband's resources.

These were the things that travelled with you: A small tin trunk, filled with baby's clothes, knitted woolen sweaters, your phulkari shawl and *chaddar*, homemade salwar kameez and embroidered chunnis. Small gold chain and two Burmese ruby rings.

From Rangoon, the capital of Burma, you all traveled in a ship called Vita to Calcutta. From there, a long train ride to Lahore. From Lahore, a truck. Then the return of the son, Grandfather Meher, to the village of Peeyan. The villagers all lit oil *diya* earthenware lamps to welcome your family "home," a home mother and father had never been to before.

To welcome them to the land of your birth, you poured oil over the threshold of your small two storied structure which your late husband's father had built. You then fetched water from the well, a well you were so proud! *Only a few farmers could afford them.* Surveying your dry fields, you knew there was much work to be done, but still, the land belonged to you from generations, and no one could take it away from you, and so, touching the dry soil to your fingertips, you placed a tilak on each of your children's forehead, on mother's and last on my round cheeked elder sister Bubbly's head. *Never forget, you belong to this land, and it belongs to you.* You lit some incense and swirled it around the small room. Soon, they would work the land and have enough to feed the family. The well in the land was gold, for water was gold in this arid land.

Mother told us years later that she had touched her swollen belly and thought: my child will be Indian.

My Other Mother

In my earliest memories, somewhere in fragmentary narratives and rumors, I remember that I was not my mother's daughter, as I didn't look anything like my mother or my sisters nor was I a typical well-behaved Punjabi girl. In the mountains of Taunggyi in the Shan States of Burma, there lived a Danu-Shan woman, my birth mother, who eked out a living by scraping the red mountain soils of her little piece of land surrounding her thatched house and growing mustard leaves and reddish. Every time five-day market came along, and the mountain women ventured down with their fresh produce—

> tender tamarind leaves for salad or soup,
> young squash flowers for stirfry or deepfry
> fermented bamboo shoots for cooking with pork
> bean paste for savory dishes
> flowers, gladioli, queen of the night, sweetpeas
> duck and chicken eggs
> fish from Inlay Lake
> and all that one could imagine
> making life savory and sweet,

—I would look longingly and searchingly in their faces for my poor birthmother who gave me away in exchange for a kilo of rice.

Hair Washing Day in Taunggyi

Sundays are hair-washing day. Today, it is cold, and the water drums set out to warm in the sun are still slightly chilly. Father, his long uncut hair washed, is sitting in the compound, reading the newspaper, and drinking hot chai. He occasionally pulls Satya's or my hair as we go by his chair, guffawing when we snatch our braids out of his teasing hands. Mother is washing clothes in the open-air bathroom. Only for washing clothes would she wear a Burmese *longyi* and a short *inji* top. Otherwise, she always wears the Punjabi *salwar kameez* with a *chunni* scarf. She is barefooted, her body small and compact. She beats the soapy clothes with a wooden stick and then, taking them between her feet, squeezes and beats them on the concrete floor before she throws them in the tub to rinse.

Knowing it was my turn to take a bath soon, I run off.

I know Mother is busy for the next hour or two, and Father is engrossed in his paper, taking time to dry his long hair, so I partly run, partly skip, still wearing my long flowery homemade dress which I sleep in—
past the goldsmith neighbor's house, where the goldsmith apprentice committed suicide by
   drinking acid for the love of a woman, star-crossed due to poverty and class differences,
      past the oak tree where I pick a few acorns—to later poke with a small needle,
         empty it of the flesh, and dry it in the sun, just for the fun of it—
            past the government high school and then the Convent School
               where I am in the 1st grade in Mother Christine's class
                  past Father's shop, PJ Singh and Brothers
                     past the closed shops on the main road
                        all the way to Indian side of town.
                           Where my uncle Amar
                           and my cousins live

Reading Byron in Burma

In the Indian side of town, I run into my uncle's wooden home and walk into my cousin's small cubbyhole of a room. He isn't there. I meander into the kitchen, and no one is there either. I wander into Amar uncle's study. He is sitting in his high-back teak chair by the open window, reading. Outside, the sun is shining, although some dark clouds are visible on the Taunggyi mountains. It is quiet. Uncle's room is filled with English books, Bryon, Keats, Shelly, Wordsworth. I love English books. Uncle's short hair is all disheveled, his round Gandhi glasses perched at the end of his long, slightly bridged nose. He is the only one in the Sikh community who dared to cut his hair even though our religion forbids it. He looks like a young and handsome Gandhi. Raising his dark and dense eyebrows at me, he smiles. "Come child, here." He pats his lap with one hand, while producing a toffee with his other, an English toffee wrapped in a gaily-colored paper. I jump up on his lap, pleased to have my favorite uncle all to myself on a Sunday morning, as I slowly unwrap the unexpected treat, popping it into my mouth, curling my tongue around it, relishing its caramel taste.

Uncle, holding the book of poems with his left hand, encircling his arm around my young body, reads softly against my cheek—"She walks in Beauty, like the night/Of cloudless climes and starry skies"—while his right hand, slowly massaging my young unformed breast, deliberately slides down towards my crotch, and only half listening to his husky and raspy voice, and sucking noisily on the toffee, now gooey, I squirm.

Born a Pisces

i am swimming among the fish
my scales are shiny, a golden glow to them
people throw pieces of fish food for me
and I clamor to the top, hungry for a piece.
the pagoda that surrounds the lake sells fish food
so people earn merit if they feed me
i have been hungry for ages; feed me,
i will bless you. see my mouth,
it is wide; we are hundreds of us waiting for your bounty.

why, that little girl is trying to hit me with her umbrella!
no one stops her but she cannot hit me, really,
for i am too fast for her little hands!

look at that massive golden Statue of Buddha
looking down upon us in this tranquil lake, Inle.

Every year before the monsoon, the monks take out the golden statue of the Buddha, *Phaundaw Oo Phaya,* and place it on a float; hundreds of Burmans line the sides in their own boats, and getting closer to the float, offer food and money to the monks.

I swim close to the statue to be blessed. One of the monks looks at me with Ko Aye Gyi's eyes and gently places a piece of sweet sticky rice for me to eat on a little leaf and, as it floats my way, I look up and see his familiar smiling golden eyes . . .

Crushed Dried Orange Peels in Homemade Curd

A childhood green and full of cherry trees with sweet-tasting springs and hanging vines from which we used to swing, skinning our arms and hands—and as we slid down the steep mountains I look at my wild brother Happy and quiet cousin, Kul—how much they resembled our father and his brothers who used to swim naked with their long hair streaming down their backs in the Shan rivers when they lived in the jungles of Shan States!

On *Pwe* or festival days, especially when the celebrations were on the mountain pagodas, Papa and the three Chachas, my father's younger brothers, would fill up huge baskets with food—whole chicken, spices, oil, salt and chili powder, onions, tomatoes, garlic, ginger, rice, potatoes, tea bags, condensed milk, plates, cups, cutlery—and inserting bamboo poles on either end at the handles, sling the them over their shoulders and take off for the mountains, Grey Stone or Yat Daw Mu, or Taung Chun. The children, all the eleven siblings and cousins, would run along with Ma, Masi, Ma's little sister who was married to my uncle Shamsher, and Laaj, our formidable but fun paternal grandma, some of us with slippers on and some without.

My slippers would invariably break, tomboy that I was, climbing trees and rocks, and then I'd skipped along barefooted. I preferred running barefoot, anyways. However, in the summer that was fine because of the tropical weather, but in the winters, because we were high up on the mountains, and nights were freezing cold, the running around barefoot would take its toll, as the skin on my toes and heel would crack and bleed. Ma would put warmed ghee with turmeric on my skin, and, when we'd bathe in the sunny afternoons, she mixed crushed dried orange peels in homemade curd and apply it on my young and skinny body.

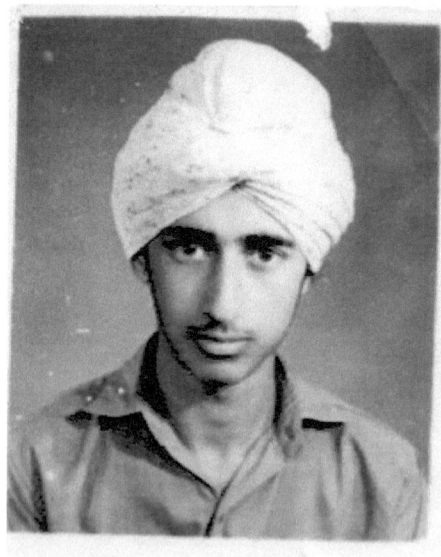

Fig. 11: Happy, the author's
older brother, circa 1961

shamed daughters

Mother had been shamed for baring too many daughters, so she was extra vigilant about raising us as "good" girls, and especially me, the unruly one. "Don't neigh like a horse!" "Don't sit with your legs spread over the arm of the chair!" (But father always does, I'd say, for which I would be rewarded with a cuff on my head).

Bubbly's skin shone like peach blossoms but mine was always cracked and peeling. My second sister Satya's skin was pale and fair, and she also had such deep brown eyes! Rina, my little sister, looked like a cherry blossom when she was small, with ruby red lips and curly hair. I was the skinny and feisty one, and didn't get too much attention from father, or for that matter, mother, as I was the third badluck daughter and forth child. My older brother, Happy, the skinny one with rapidly blinking eyes and swift intermittent sniffs, was the apple of Laaj's eyes. Satya was tolerated by Laaj, especially as she was so softspoken with a voice, according to Laaj, "like a koel" who brought along Happy. And Rina, although another unwanted daughter, stole my father's heart with her perfect face and almond eyes, and Laaj forgave her for she brought along a little brother, the last of the siblings, little Manjit, the winner of hearts! I had not been so lucky nor so auspicious! Manjit was beautiful with long eyelashes and long lustrous hair and became the one who sat on a red throne on my parents' hearts.

Mother always asked me to do the chores, but not Rina or my sister Satya, saying Rina was too small, Satya to weak, and as for Bubbly, the scholar, she was too busy studying for her exams at the Convent School. So, whenever I found an opportunity, I would challenge Rina to a boxing match and would box her ears soundly, but she would always sit on my skinny body, as she was round and plump and could always throw me down, even though I was three years older than her. She scratched my face many times, always leaving single or double nail impressions so that my skin looked like a Mughal hunting painting.

Fig. 12: The author, Jaspal Kaur Singh, standing on the extreme left of the frame with younger sister, Rina, and three cousins, Kuldip's siblings and Shamsher's children in front of the Avocado Tree, circa 1957

Kul, the Keeper of Secrets

My earliest memories of Taunggyi are of the thatch house that we lived in on the other side of the Government school. It was built on bamboo stilts and had a bamboo verandah, where Mother and Meeto Masi sat, and scrubbed dishes clean with bits of coconut husk and wood ash. My cousin Kul and I ran around under the house or scrambled into the fields surrounding the area and picked pink and blue wildflowers. We would break the necks of flowers until the stamens showed and then linked them all to make garlands or earring. Mother said we looked like like two *balungareys*, little puppies, scrambling around, as we were inseparable. Kul was the gentle one and I, I was rough and loud, and he followed me around without questions, so we got along well.

Kul was the keeper of my secrets. When Kumar Sharma, the fourteen-year-old schoolboy, took me aside while we played next door when I was just five, and peeled off my homemade knickers, touching my bottom, saying, "Let's play a new game, just you and I," Kul watched. But when Kumar Sharma took me a few days later to the collapsed government school building, Kul went and told Bubbly, who, along with mother, followed us to the school. Kumar Sharma told me to sit up on the desk. He took my bloomers off and touched my vagina. They rushed him and beat him with the stick. He scurried off. They dragged me off. Mother held my hand tight, pulling me behind her, but Bubby called me "Besharam." Shameless. Shocked and frightened, for I didn't know what I had done wrong, seeing the big stick in mother's hand and her angry face, I cried all the way home, looking at Kul with sad eyes.

The next day, Kul asked me to show him my special game with Kumar Sharma.

Fig. 13: Kuldip Singh and Jaspal Kaur Singh, circa 1953

Fig. 14: Jaspal Kaur Singh and Kuldip Singh, circa 1955

Love Stories

I was born in the Son Born Hospital—the third daughter and fourth child, wedged between three siblings on top and two siblings below—and I called myself "the middle." But somehow, I never thought of myself as being dead center. I was always finding amusing things for the others to laugh at, more a middle comedian. I never thought of myself as a bridge. But, decades later, I became one, a bridge and a storyteller.

My older sisters sent me on errands to the market. They said I was nosey because I asked them why they needed fermented fish or fried cicadas or why they had soiled their *shalwars* on a monthly basis. I had to wait years to figure out most of these on my own.

They scared me with rumors of blood pouring from between my legs. A period is what they called it. Not a full stop. My friend Surjeet from first grade had some information about it but a period—not what was at the end of a sentence—bled down a girl's legs. It was not a satisfactory answer. Even more mysterious and fascinating was her talk about parents joined together like dogs in the street. She said it was love.

At the convent school we attended we were taught western morals and learned about love through the stories we read. I asked mother what love was. She said she didn't know. Does she love me, I asked? She laughed.

a period at the end of a life

My sisters, fed up of my nosey questions as they called it, and wanting privacy to read their love stories in their room, whispered me away to our Inda neighbor's poor cousin and maid, Ma Nyo, who fed me leftover Inda food, *laphet tot*, fried tofu, fish in green chili sauce, crushed peanut *hin, ngape* and *hin kha* soup, and vignettes from her village for my growing imagination. She'd tell me tales of Inle Lake, the largest lake in Asia, and stories of lake dwellers, and about her family, especially Donald, tall and gangly with shaggy hair, her far-off cousin and our neighbors and her employer's son.

When I was fourteen, I had the biggest crush on Donald, with his Beatle-cut hairstyle and cowboy boots. He was tall and lanky, and I thought he looked like a character from one of the love stories we'd read, my sister Satya and me. Before the discovery of Mills and Boone novels, my sisters read from what was called "love story picture library." These were novellas with pictures. Satya taught me to love stories and tales. She taught me to love poetry and songs. Each time I read one of the love stories, I thought of how skinny Donald was.

After the military coup of 1962, after father lost his business and home, and we were displaced as stateless refugees to India, after Donald's family lost their jewelry store, and after he became a drug addict, as many of our friends and family members did, he became extra skinny. He died when he was just 24.

Fig. 15: Satya, Bally, and Bubbly in Rangoon, circa 1961

English Morals

Burping was a cardinal sin and was discouraged by my sisters and, they would say, the nuns would call you savage if you did. So was farting. We didn't care. At the age of fifteen, Bubbly dictated to us these cardinal sins. She'd beat and pinch us until our arms or legs blued—most of the time we escaped her punishments. Kul would cup his hands, pretend to fart into them, then act as if releasing the foul smell in front of my fastidious eldest sister's nose and run away as fast as he could.

One day I tried the trick on her, and she got me, though. She pinched and twisted my forearm, and when I wriggled and flailed my long arms, she whacked me on my head. Struggling wildly, I inadvertently cracked my elbow on her lips and her mouth swelled up. Next day, Kul and I laughed at Bubbly and said she looked like Nanda, an Indian actress with fleshy lips. She chased us with a leather slipper in hand, but we disappeared behind the kitchen into the Son Born Hospital compound.

Bubbly soon budded into a sexy, sensual animal though—and all the family fears rested on her shoulders and her Marilyn Monroe-like breasts. One of my mother's cousins had eloped with a young Sikh man when she was sixteen. She was brought back home but she had broken her father's heart, who died within the month. So, as my mother watched us girls, we watched Bubbly becoming a game for the entire family—some of us watched in fun, some in admiration and emulation, some in dismay, and some in trepidation, but there were some, like our Uncle Shamsher and Amar, the Byron-loving uncle, who hoped that she would be the one to bring the Singh name down. They said, "Bubbly is the who would blacken your nose, Joth!"

Fig. 16: The author, Jaspal Kaur Singh, with classmate, Margaret Haigh and sister, Rina, circa 1964

Broken Heart

Our new house sits a little high in the Forest Quarters, kitty-corner from the Income Tax Office and opposite to the Income Tax officer's house, away from the Indian part of town. The garden that Laaj plants, full of jasmine vines, dahlias, roses, and gladioli, is surrounded by blue jacarandas, avocadoes, plums, pine, and oak trees. Behind the kitchen in a patch of land, she grows corn, chayote squash, chili, cilantro, and tomatoes. She says she remembers her father's farm in British India in the far reaches of Punjab where she used to live until the age of thirteen. Although the fields were mostly green and productive in the spring, they became dry and dusty in the winters, so they barely had enough to eat as they had so many mouths to feed in the family. Plus, the taxes were so high!

Laaj was married off early to my grandfather Meher and came to live with him in far off Burma. As a young bride, she says she used to dream of the Burmese *nats*, the greenghosts, the spirits of those whose lives were violently cut off in their prime, and the Shan cannibals, but over the years, she mostly forgot about those ideas. When Laaj was newly married, Meher used to work as a driver's apprentice, a spare, for his maternal uncle's transport business. His uncle had two lorries and they went back and forth from Rangoon to Delhi carrying Indianmade goods, such as cloth, lanterns, and bicycles, and other perishable products, such a pulses and grains, for the local markets.

Laaj missed Meher every day, so now she tried to recreate the feeling of a Punjabi farm in the little patch behind our house, planting okras and bitter melons, which Meher used to love, especially when she stuffed them with crushed onions, garlic, ginger, spices, a piece of tamarind, and shallow fry them on the *tava* on low heat for hours until they were crisp and golden. He would eat them with the fresh rotis that she used to puff on the slow burning ambers and then smeared each one with a dollop of white homemade butter. That was a while back, before WWII, before the 1947 Partition of India, before they lost everything, before Meher died of a broken heart.

Fig. 17: Gurdeep Kaur, a classmate, and the author, Jaspal Kaur Singh, circa 1963

bamboo shack

Our Taunggyi home was not so lush and solid before I was born in 1951. Laaj and Meher, along with their first born, my father Joth, and his brother, Shamsher, used to live in the little bamboo shack behind Meher's small shop on main road, next to the beer bars, and in front of the small Sikh temple. Grandmother Laaj often tells me about the small place, how they all slept in crammed quarters behind the shop. It was there, she said, on the main road, near all the Indian community members, many of them petty traders, tailors, and street cleaners, that her sons grew up, speaking Burmese and Shan, their Punjabi stilted and odd to her ears.

Evening Walks with Laaj

Joth and Shamsher were enrolled at the American Baptist Mission School through the help of their priest at the Gurudwara where they learned to speak yet another language, English. But their education was disrupted due to the Japanese occupation of Burma in 1942. To add to their many tongues, which Grandmother Laaj has a hard time deciphering, they added the Japanese language taught to them by the Japanese occupier at their schools. She loathed the Japanese soldiers, who were mean and rough with Joth and Shamsher, but were particularly horrible to Meher at his shop. Most time, she used to tell us, they would take things without paying for them, often beating him senseless. Once, she said to me on our evening walk around the Taunggyi water reservoir by the mountain: *Palo, I try not to remember those terrible days, but they often creep into my dreams! Meher wakes me up, saying, Laaj, Laaj, you are safe. Sub theek hai!*

Son Born Hospital

My mother Tej, newly married to my father, Joth, used to cook in the little kitchen with a wood stove in their home behind the shop. The stove was constructed of mud and cow dung mixed with chopped up gunny sack smeared on to three big concrete blocks. My older sister, Bubbly, was born during the Japanese occupation of Burma. Even though she was a girl, Grandmother Laaj made a big show of making sweets and distributing it to our relatives to celebrate the birth, but when I was born a few years later, the third badluck daughter, Laaj refused to visit my mom, who was at the unsuitably named "Son Born Hospital" to see me for almost a week. She said she had felt redeemed at least because my brother, Happy, was born a few years after Satya, my second elder sister's arrival, so she could lift her head up in the Sikh community by celebrating his arrival with not only *laddoos* and *punjeeri*, but she even got a *halwai* to make fresh *jalebees* for the Indian community! But not at my birth, oh no! There was only silence and mourning broken by my lusty cries, as I was born fat and chubby, my mother's largest and healthiest baby.

Fig. 18: Tej Kaur with the author, Jaspal Kaur Singh, in her arms, circa 1951 in Taunggyi

Bubbly Bubbles and Glows

We have a special bond, Bubbly, or Bubbles, as I often called her, and I, as she used to pay special attention to me, for both our *chi*, according to her, are strong. She literally bubbles and glows as we walk to school, her long braid swinging behind her rounded buttocks, her cheeks deep pink, her eyes dark-brown with long fringes, sparking like the mountain brook after monsoon rain near Lover's Lane, and I see admiring eyes looking at her. She said we are like our father, Joth, who, when he was a young boy, got his long uncut hair stuck to the mud at the bottom of the muddy river, but even though he was thought dead, he reappeared after a while from the depth of the murky waters, transformed. He grew up fast, and wise, with an extra strong chi after that moment. Bubbly said we, she and I, both take after him. Shamsher, she said, has a weak chi. And Happy, I asked? *"He is a mixture of both Joth and Tej, a strong chi, which he inherited from Joth, and a calm and quiet chi, which he inherited from Tej, our soft-spoken mother"*. Satya? *"Like Tej, weak but calm chi,"* she said.

Fig. 19: Bubbly, circa 1956

A Sikh Coolie in the Indian National Army

In 1946, my parents fled from Burma to Punjab in India, but had to return during the Partition after Satya was born. Their flight occurred due to the Japanese occupation of Burma from 1942 to 1945 during WWII. A year after Bubbly was born, Joth and Tej, tired, hungry, and fed-up from hiding in the jungles of Shan States due to the constant bombing by the Allied Army on the Japanese occupied Burma, allowed Grandmother Laaj to persuaded them to go to Punjab back to her old home in Rawalpindi. Tej was pregnant again. The Japanese had been brutal to all the Burmese people during the occupation. Joth and Meher were mistreated by the soldiers. Shamsher had to march with the Japanese and with Netaji Subas Chandra Bose's Indian National Army for many awful and brutal months during the 1944 Quit India Movement.

When he was just nineteen years old during WWII, Shamsher was recruited by Bose, the leader of the Indian National Army who beseeched all the sons of Mother India, particularly the first born in Burma, to free India from British rule. Netaji Bose made his fiery speech in Burma and asked Indians to march to Delhi to fight the Brits—*Delhi Chalo!* The Japanese coerced or forced, one way or the other, the sons of India in Taunggyi and other parts of Burma to march to India. Joth said, *I owe Shamsher.*

Shamsher became a *coolie* for the Japanese and Indian officers. He would often describe to us the torturous hikes in the jungles with heavy loads on his back while the Japanese or Indian officers prodded him as if he were a donkey, especially if they thought he was slacking off. He returned home after the bombing in Hiroshima and Nagasaki, exhausted, sick, demoralized, and unnerved. If the US had not dropped the nuclear bombs on Hiroshima and Nagasaki, where thousands upon thousands of Japanese people died, Shamsher felt he would still have been marching and carrying loads for them in the jungles!

Satya, the Truth

It was in 1946 when Meher, along with Grandmother Laaj and the family, arrived at his hometown in Punjab, Peeyan.

But after Satya, my second older sister, small and colicky, was born, Hindu Muslim violence and slaughter began due to the imminent Partition of India, and they had to run for their lives in the middle of the night in early 1947. They heard the roar of *Allah hu Akbar, Har Har Mahadev* and *Jo Bole So Nihal* followed by torturous cries through many nights while they cowered in their grain room. Laaj, my parents with two small children, my uncle Shamsher, had to walk for miles in the middle of the night. Meher refused to leave his home and stayed back, but Joth had to go back with an army truck and rescue him a few days later, as many Sikhs were already slaughtered in the melee. Meher was hidden in a grain storeroom by his Muslim neighbors and was thankfully safe, although he never recovered from the violence he witnessed nor from losing his home, once again. A few days later, as they were leaving Lahore, their train was attacked as men threw rocks and rattled their doors and windows, but miraculously, or so they told us, they escaped safely all the way back to Burma. They lost their home and friends and left with only their two small children and a couple of bundles of valuable things. Laaj carried the key to her house for decades, mourning her lost home, her locked truck with her good woolen shawls, embroidered *phulkari* bedspreads and *chunnis* which she had handwoven and handstitched as a young bride, and her few good silver dishes. Tej carried her children—and almost lost one when Satya dropped from her nerveless fingers and hands—and the few warm sweaters she had knitted and three salwar kameez she had stitched for her daughters. Shamsher stumbled on the small whimpering figure, picked her up and carried her the rest of the way. *Did Tej mean to leave Satya, her colicky second daughter, behind in Punjab?* Joth carried a small cloth bundle with the few bits of jewelry they had and a couple of thousand rupees.

Meher couldn't work after they arrived back in Burma due to ill health. It was up to Joth as the elder son to became responsible for all of them and he promised never to leave Burma again, as long as he lived. He managed to build a small shack in the main road of Taunggyi and began trading again. He sold a few pieces of mother and grandmother's jewelry and took off to the border of China and Thailand, purchasing goods to sell in the five-day market in Taunggyi. Meher, who left with empty hands, started to drink heavily, succumbed to depression, and died soon after due, as Laaj would say, to his shattered kismet.

Jaati and *Paati*

My very first home was built mostly of bamboo with wooden stilts where the Shan winds blew from the mountains to the deck below the house during brutal winters. Some nights, I woke up to wild dogs, which I could see below between the wooden slats of the floor of the house, howling. My cousin Kul, Shamsher's first born and my agemate, and I used to hide under there during hot summer days. We could hear Ma and the beautiful Meeto Masi, my mother's little sister married to Shamsher, complaining about Grandmother Laaj and her constant comparison of them to other higher caste Sikh women in the community. *What a fraud Laaj is, believing in jaati and paati and dares to call herself a Sikh!*

Fig. 20: Tej Kaur with her sister, Meeto, in front of her and Gurmat Kaur, her sister-in-law next to her, circa 1961

bakri, the badluck daughter

Many years after I was born, we moved to a beautiful home with the cemented lower half, a wooden second floor, and a tin roof! Ma constructed another woodstove from cow dung, chopped gunny sack and mud and three concrete blocks. We used to burn wood to cook our food on clay pots. Ma and Meeto Masi use the ash from the woodstove to scrub pots, pans, and dishes with coconut husk. I, the third badluck daughter, was always roped in to wash the dishes in the cold water, or to crush onions, garlic, and ginger in the stone mortar and pestle for the daily curries.

Today, as I sit in the tiny kitchen crushing the ingredients, I mutter under my breath—*why don't you ask Bubbly to wash the dishes? Why don't you ask Satya to crush the onions?* I already know her answer, *oh, but Bubbly has so much homework as she is in the nineth grade. And Satya, she is so frail and weak.* Ma, gentle but mostly exhausted from the daily household chores, hears me muttering, and managing a slight laugh, calls me a goat, a *bakri*! *Why a goat, of all the creatures, I mutter!* Chuckling, she says, "Because you, who help me the most, are like a goat who provides us milk, but who always manage to shit in the same bucket! *Bak, bak, bak!*" It's true, I do help Ma with the household chores, ironing clothes, washing dishes, sweeping the floor, but that's because I'm always hovering around her for attention while Bubbly goes off reading novels or playing basketball and Satya sings songs in the garden! And Ma always praises them, saying: what a good scholar she is! What a sweet voice! So, when I crush the onions, I pound real hard, and mutter under my breath, scattering the onions and garlic on the floor, or sweeping the dirt from one room to another, sometimes scattering the dust all over the house! *Bakri, indeed!*

Slackers

Every month, a lorry-load of wood is delivered to our house. Papa would pay a few kyats to the brawny tattooed Pa'O men who'd come down from the mountains on market day looking for odd jobs to have them chop up the wood for us. We children would then stack them in the woodshed. If we'd slack off when stacking them, we get a caning from Shamsher, the self-proclaimed disciplinarian of the family. The ones Shamsher felt slacked off (do we really slack off or he thinks we do, like the Japanese and Indian army officers thought he did! Huh!)—would be lined up against the garage door. It was mostly me, the muttering child and third useless daughter, or my brother, Happy, the star and light of the Singh family who would bear the brunt of his anger, especially if he could not locate Bubbly, his special target. Shamsher told my mother he found Bubbly, as compared to the dainty Satya, too feisty and too bold, wearing brightly colored dresses and makeup, or even worse, slack pants, ostensibly to practice basketball at her school, St. Anne's Convent, but he was sure of it, to flirt with Donald, or Ko Ko Aung, or what's his name, Victor! *Those guitars twanging convent high school boys who think they are Elvis Presley, or worse still, the Beatles! Sickening! He was fed up of it! All this English Shinglish teaching, he'd say! It's going to ruin us!*

Netaji Subas Chandra Bose and a debt owed

Today, it is Sunday, so I loiter around Ma and Meeto Masi, who are preparing dinner in the tiny kitchen behind our house. I was roped in to help them, as usual. After I finished crushing the onions, garlic, and ginger for the curry, I, along with Kul, Happy, Satya and Bubbly, help stack the chopped wood in the woodshed. I hate it because I always manage to get splinters in my hands, but Bubbly and Happy are good and swift. Kul and Satya mostly pick the small pieces, but they get away with minimum work, somehow. Bubbly sings, "*Chahey koi mujhe jungle kahay!*" in her loud voice, as she had just seen Shammi Kapoor's film, *Junglee*, a few weeks ago. Satya's sweet and melodious voice soon accomplices Bubbly's lusty notes. Happy follows with a loud, *yahoo!* We all laugh, trying to imitate Shammi Kapoor.

Shamsher, who had been in his room above the back veranda resting after his lunch, suddenly appears and catches hold of Bubbly, slams her against the woodshed door, lifts her skirt up, exposing her flowered homemade panties—the one sewed by Ma. My Nana, a tailor, taught Ma when she was just a little girl of nine how to sew. I love Bubbly's mauve flower-patterned panties, as mine are plain and ugly. Grandmother Laaj hates it when Ma makes beautiful things on her Singer sewing machine for us, making sure to taunt my mother about her tailoring caste. "I belong to the Arora caste, a merchant caste, which is much higher than your mother's." Bubbly would yell at Laaj: *Sikhs don't believe in the caste system*, but Laaj, who is so agile for someone her age, would leap up to her feet and chase Bubbly, saying, *rukja, shaitan!* But at this moment, Bubbly is like a statue, frozen in place by a fear or hatred so strong, she acts and looks dead! Shamsher whacks the Slazenger badminton racquet on her flowered panties, her buttocks, and thighs. Satya and I cringe and mutter, calling him a *shaitan*, but we are all too afraid of him to openly confront him. Ma, who is cooking in the kitchen, which is housed in a little hut next to the woodshed and separated from our house by a little drain, hears him, and sprinting up to Shamsher, wrestles the racquet from his skinny, but strong hands, and yells at him to stop—*bus karo!* Shamsher, still angry, but aware of her sharp voice, surprisingly backs off, and Ma, dragging the stoic but bruised Bubbly to her room, carefully applies soothing salve on her bruised skin, saying, *why doesn't he ever hit his own son, Kul? Why my children, for Waheguru's sake?* Bubbly's dark eyes are staring out the window to the far-off mountains, her lashes damp, and she says to Ma, *one day I will show him.*

That evening when Joth returns from the shop, Ma complains to him about Shamsher, but all he says is, *Shamsher learned the discipline as a soldier from the late Netaji Subas Chandra Bose when he was in The Indian National Army, and from the British who taught him the adage: "Spare the rod and spoil the child" in the American Baptist Mission school. He is just doing his duty by us and teaching our children discipline and morality. Never forget, he took my place in Netaji Subas Bose' Indian National army and suffered for our sakes. I owe him. We owe him.*

Turmeric Marinated Fried Sparrows

Shamsher devised infinite ways of punishing me, my older brother Happy, and sister Bubbly (while my cousin, Kul, and my sister, Satya, for some reason, always manage to evade the punishment)—a caning for failing exams on our bare buttocks, leather thong sandals slapping our backs for returning the gaze, the look of insolence, he calls it; the Slazenger badminton racquet for special occasions, such as being sly, eating street food behind his back or being too bold, staying out after dark with friends, or simply his open palm, a big one for a tall and skinny man, for not completing our homework.

It was a rule in our house when I was just a girl of nine that each exam failed would result in one hard stroke of the cane, and if you failed two exams, you would get two strokes of the cane, canes that were solid wood, an inch thick, the kind that English fabric from Manchester, England, used to come rolled in for my father's clothing store. The store, PJ Singh and Brothers on the main road of Taunggyi in the Shan States of Burma, became the staging ground for many of the punishment scene as both brothers spent most of their daytime there.

At twenty-six, Shamsher was thin and tall, a sparse beard covering most of his hawknosed face, shaggy eyebrows, and small penetrating eyes. He always wore a dark blue turban. He seldom smiled. The back of our bare buttocks and thighs remembered the texture of the pine wooden stick, imprinted in our memories. To cane a child had little logic in my mind but Shamsher believed in the rod—and the sound of it on our naked flesh. He had learned it from English books read at the American Baptist Mission School in Taunggyi.

Also, if a beating for bad grades or failing classes wasn't done, the father was seen as a soft touch, a failure, unable to groom his children for the medical field or the sciences within the small Indian community in Burma. Our father, Joth, was a loving parent who seldom caned our thighs. He was the one who played funny tricks, swimming underwater and pulling our legs, splashing us when we went to the mountain spring for picnics. He had a loud laugh. And merry eyes. Shamsher, on the other hand, who only passed grade eight as compared to our father who had matriculated, resented the fact that he had to stop his education due to the Second World War; he was too old to go back to school and never let us forget how fortunate we were to attend an English school. Grim faced, he told our father that he would see to our success in life. Father, whose application to the medical school in Rangoon, the capital of Burma, hung between the British colonial regime and the colonized Burma for a long period, reluctantly acquiesced to uncle's unorthodox logic and methods.

Joth often apologized to Shamsher for his limitations, thanking him for disciplining his children, and with a stick in his hand, Shamsher showed him how to raise it almost to his ear and swing it through the air. This demonstration often went on for hours. Between customers, and after the noon-lunch hour, when the day would become languid, the stick, swung almost in slow motion by Shamsher, will rustle long sleeves of imported fabric shirts or swoosh around the long hand-woven cotton sarongs, as through writhing in anticipation of the actual procedure on our bodies. Joth, a reluctant learner, re-adjusted the garments in loving details, running his hands over the imported fabric, terylene, marveling at the synthetic fiber, so smooth, unlike the rough cotton, so easy to wash and wear.

My older brother, Happy, awkward, gawky at the age of fourteen, yet still oddly daring, having quietly grown a mustache and a shadow of a beard, with his long uncut hair, washed and loosened on Sundays, ventured into the woods and surrounding mountains. His hawknosed face with beaming eyes masked his awkwardness, and whenever girls stared at him, he tried to show off. He would balance his catapult on his palm, taking out the rolled and dried pellets made from river mud from his pocket to use as projectiles to hunt, and acting nonchalant, would stretch the rubber to its limit. But he had a nervous tic. He blinked his eyes rapidly while sniffling loudly. For these minor disorders, he earned the name of a water buffalo from Shamsher, a *chwai!* We hated the name, but somehow, it stuck.

Happy roamed the streets as well as the jungles with his friends, shooting sparrows, pigeons, rabbits with his homemade catapult, and sometimes raiding the corner shop for *baya chaw*, the fried spicy vegetable fritters that the vender sold every evening before dinner. The mountains of Shan States, far from the lowlands of Rangoon and Mandalay, were lush and dense and one could disappear in it for hours on end.

Summer days were long.

We children roamed the woods or the many local bazaars, sneaking forbidden street food, as Shamsher thought it was unhygienic—such a snob! —or simply sit in groups, telling stories with the neighborhood children. When Happy would return with two or three sparrows, the bigger birds, like pigeons, having eluded him, I would pluck, gut, and marinade the birds in turmeric and salt, deep-fry them in mother's kitchen, sharing the little legs and wings with Happy and his friends, sitting under the avocado tree, crunching on crispy meat.

Happy was failing all his classes.

Shamsher noted.

That year, when I was in the third grade, I failed two subjects. I was already behind in school, the nuns having kept me back for five years in kindergarten, labeling me as a slow learner. Shamsher told me to bare my bottom so he could get the maximum effect out of the stick. I had to bend at the waist on top of the wooden dining table and he grunted in a breathless way when he struck. My homemade bloomers pulled down, my head touching the table, I was a table display, the edge of it cutting my tender tummy. A bird. My half-remembered memories of spiders roaming my body while Shamsher stroked it with his stick visited me for many years in early dawns.

Happy was caned next, as if Shamsher wanted to tend to the work all at once.

My sisters Bubbly and Satya, who passed all their exams, and I, peeked from the crack in the dining room door like accomplices, listening to the loud noise of a stick hitting him, *thraak, thraak*. Happy, wild eyed from unshed tears, his *joora*, his top knot, undone, his long uncut hair framing his flushed face. Mother, breath escaping in small bursts, standing by the dining room door, stared hard at my father, who, moist eyed muttered, "It is for his own good. Spare the rod and spoil the child." My mother's body was trembling. She didn't understand the meaning of his words, but she hissed, "May his bones be infested with maggots!"

Happy laid stretched out on the table, quiet as a church mouse.

Joth and Shamsher walked out for their evening stroll into the heat.

That night calls of birds mimicking our cries meandered through the open windows while sudden monsoon rain clattered on our tin rooftop, the din entering our sleeping brains, coiled around our bodies and skin, snakelike.

Fig. 21: Prab Joth Singh and Shamsher Singh in front of the Sikh Gurudwara in Taunggyi, circa 1959

Fig. 22: Shamsher Singh and Prab Joth Singh, circa 1961

Greasy Indians

I was in kindergarten. I was only five years old. It happened this way. Every day at lunch time, we would walk home for our meals. Our home was about eight minutes from school, so my cousin Kul and I would walk back together. After lunch of dal and rice or rice and *channa* curry or rice and *rajmah* curry, we would walk back to class.

That one time, I forgot my school bag at home. Preety Das, the Anglo-Indian teacher, asked me where my book was. I looked for my bag and not seeing it on my desk, and feeling petrified, pointed to Khin Khin, sitting next to me, and said, she took it. Pretty Das ordered me to come to the front of the class, and taking a long stick, asked me to hold out my hand. My face red with shame and my body shaking with fear, I tentatively held out my right hand. She brought the stick hard on my hands and arm and then asked me for the other hand and struck it and then, as if possessed, lifted my skirt in the back, exposing my homemade bloomers, and whipped my bottom and my thighs and calves. I jumped, shaken and in immense pain, and cried. Snot ran out of my nose into my mouth. As I was hiccupping, she said, "Now go, go and get your bag from your home." I ran out of the class, out of the massive gray stone gates with their iron grilled topped with the signboard, St. Anne's Convent High School, fused onto the carved arches, past the pine trees which always whispered in the Taunggyi winds, past the Taunggyi library, past Asa Singh uncle's general store, all the way to PJ Singh and Brothers' shop, right into father and uncle standing by the stalls in front of the shop. Father's face turned purple in anger at the welts rising on my arms and legs, and taking my hands, marched me back to school right into Mother Superior's office. In halting English, he explained to her that Pretty Das had punished me for forgetting my bag at home in such a brutal manner. Mother Superior, who was used to us kids being beaten all the time, still had the grace to look a bit contrite at the welts on my arms and legs. She apologized on behalf of Pretty, saying she will reprimand the teacher. Father left me in the good hands of Mother Superior who summoned Mother Christine, an Anglo nun, the kindergarten school supervisor. I quaked in my shabby leather shoes, for Mother Christine was the one who always barked order for us at the morning assembly to sing our "Our Father" and "Come Boly Gos" in a louder voice. She always had a stick in her hands and would whip boys and girls into shape almost every morning. But when she came that day, she was all smiles; she called me Miss PJ. I looked around to see who she was referring to, as I had never heard myself called that. I thought, okay, she must mean me as daughter of my father, PJ Singh, or Prob Joth Singh. She took me by my hand and led me to the music room. She got me a shiny hard candy with sugar crystals sprinkled on it. I loved the candy, dreaming of England and cakes. I sat by the piano, hoping someday to play or sing, or being in a stage show as my sister Satya had been, playing the role of little dolls as the song, "dolls for sale," sung by one of the cute Anglo boys rang out to the audience. I dreamed of playing an Indian doll with my red salwar kameez and shiny chunni.

When I returned to class in the evening, Pretty Das ignored me. A week later, I was taking private tuitions from her at her home. I would steal little soaps and candy from my father's shop and take it to her in the evening. She became really kind to me. She smiled at me. She asked me where I got the soap or candy from and if my father was aware of the items. I lied and said, yes.

A few years later, my teacher Ruby Haight, an Anglo-Burmese and my close friend Maragaret's mother, yelled and screamed at me, saying, you Indians are so stupid! Was I just stupid? Was I someone who didn't know how to learn or read or understand math? I was one of the oldest students in class. At home, father and mother cared about homework for Bubbly, Satya and especially, my older brother, Happy, but me, the fourth child and unlucky girl, got away with clowning around and entertaining everyone. Kul, being the first son of my uncle, always did well in school as his father took extra care with his books and homework. I, along with my younger, but beautiful sister, Reena, simply played when we would be forced to sit down to complete our homework. Reena was lucky and blessed, because her beauty stole our father's heart, even though she was the fourth daughter. She never studied. In Kindergarten, Mother Christine would lead me from class to class along with two other students, one a daughter of a domestic worker, one the son of a converted Christian shop salesman, with dunce caps and STUPID written on them on our heads. We laughed along with the other students who made fun of us. I thought it was extra funny with the caps on, but deep down, I felt something that I was not able to articulate till years later, a sense of unease, a sense of discomfort, as I could tell Mother Christine was having an especially triumphant time. She was an Anglo, and she always told us how superior the Europeans were and how lazy we Indians and Burmese were, especially us greasy ones.

Fig. 23: Jaspal Kaur Singh, sitting in front on the right side of the frame with her schoolmates, Molly on the left, Polly behind her and Surjit Kaur on the left of the frame, circa 1963 in Taunggyi

Fig. 24: Khin Myint Mu, the author's best friend in high school, with whom she was finally reunited after more than 30 years in Taunggyi in 1997. Photo circa 1967.

Fig. 25: The author, Jaspal Kaur Singh, circa 1966, as a highschooler, a few years before she was exiled from Burma as a refugee.

Fig. 26: Manjit, my youngest brother, circa 1963

Taunggyi Dreamscapes (A Return to a Mythical Home)

Memories of Taunggyi are as misty as spring rain:
1. of morning walks in the hills
2. of fried tofu salad wrapped in banana leaves
3. of Ma's scallion and turmeric fried rice and fermented fish curry
4. of tennis lessons at Taunggyi club with American coaches
5. of Shan, Kachin, Chinese, Indians, Inda, Pa'O, Karin classmates
6. of European nuns in pristine habits
7. of day scholars at Saint Anne's Convent High School
8. of wanting to be like the Christian teachers and students, so Santa Claus will also love and visit me
9. of caning, dunce hats, sexual awakenings
10. of military terror, rights stolen, friends parting, families dislocated like green ants
11. of shattering love's desire and dreams
12. of poverty, midnight military raids, farewells in the early starry morning as crushed ice under bare feet
13. of crying childhood friends at railway station's platform, splitting of familiar places, longings for unknown legendary places, wanting to belong, to re-turn, to gaze ahead like lost doe in moonlight
15. of fearing laws and unknown systems of India, re-learning, night and day, to re-remember lost culture and customs, tongues split, heart loaded, like hump on camel's back in Thar Desert
14. of being eternally mistaken and of being mistook, of being misrecognized as foreigners, as "imported" like dates from Basra
15. of seeking dark shadowy places, disco nights of this or that, wanting to call Delhi home in crocheted spaces, a Delhi, which having been conquered and looted for centuries, didn't know what belonging meant.

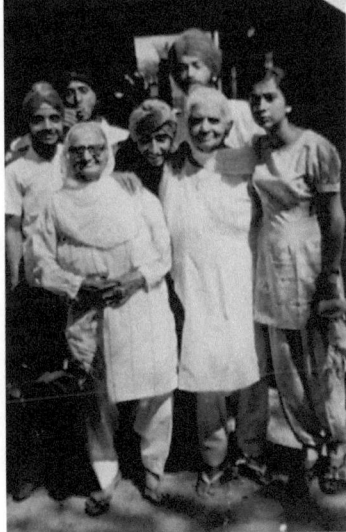

Fig 27: The author's two grandmothers, Nani Bishan Kaur (on the left side of the frame in front) and Dadi Laaj Kaur (on Nani's right) with their grandchildren, circa 1980 in New Delhi, India

Red Lipstick, Red Pumps

Bubbly started wearing red lipstick and red pumps when she was in high school and was called a slut by my mother's younger sister, Meeto Masi. Bubbly and Satya wore saris and makeup; they careered around our house in high heels, and even ventured outside to the street, trying to walk a straight line, Masi said, to boys.

Meeto and Shamsher, one luscious and the other a humorless stick of a man, married to each other through my grandmother's persistence and sweet syrupy talk with my maternal grandparents, said: "Satya looks like an angel but the other, Bubbly for sure, is a slut in her lipstick the color of blood—one is a red rose and the other a red hot chili."

Was the color of blood a portent of other losses in our lives?

Laaj's Garden

Grandmother Laaj had creative and nurturing hands. She could cook flavorful dishes and grow dreamy plants and flowers. Her lush bushes of roses, zinnias and dahlias attracted those who yearned for color and a certain wildness in beauty. Her queen of the night bush attracted even the cobra to our yard!

We planted an avocado seed in the dark rich soil. Its plainness looked out of place. But we watered it every day. Satya and I helped, but the tree, when it began to flower and bear fruit, became known as Satya's tree.

Back in Taunggyi at the Convent School, I used to say to the nuns that my favorite flowers were Iris, although I had never seen one in my entire life. In India, I crafted Iris silk flowers, but only later in life, much later, did I learn that my favorite flowers are actually lotus with their colorful pink petals and large green traylike leaves floating in the water.

In 2001, when I visited China to teach at the University of Guangxi, a nun at a Buddhist temple divined my fate, calling me a lotus blossom, who, although immersed in a burning fire, continues to bloom.

Fig. 28: The author, Jaspal Kaur Singh, on the extreme right of the frame in the first row, sitting next to best friend Khin Myin Mu, at a wedding in Taunggyi, circa 1967

Shirley's ghost

Satya and I miss Bubbly every day. I am in the sixth grade and Satya is in the first year at Taunggyi College. Satya, such a good student, wanted to go to the Rangoon University, like Bubbly, but after she broke her ankle in a freak accident, she remained home and goes to the local college. She was on a school trip to Mandalay to see the Glass Palace when her bus hit a black pig. Being small boned as it is, and so frail, it took her months to mend. Therefore, Mother was reluctant to send her far off to Rangoon and, lucky for me, I have at least one older sister near me who teaches me to love English songs, poetry, and novels.

Bubbly left for Rangoon to become a doctor when she was eighteen soon after she passed her matric exam. Whenever she comes home during her summer breaks, I feel like I don't recognize her. She shows us fancy dance steps, like the Cha Cha or Twist. Her classmates, who are with her at Rangoon university, sometimes visit our home. They are all so elegant, speaking in a kind of city Burmese that Satya and I try to emulate.

Bubbly changes so much, especially after the 1962 military coup and Ne Win's Burmese Road to Socialism. On the 7th of July 1962, she had taken part in the student demonstration against Ne Win's rule. It was gunned down and dozens of students were slaughtered. She had managed to escape with Aung Gyi, her classmate. He had literally dragged her from the scene, as she had stood there shattered and shocked. The next day, the military blew up their student union building—RUSU, the Rangoon University Student Union—and the army buried students' bodies in shallow graves around Rangoon. When classes temporarily resumed, she was stunned, she tells us, to see the body of her Chinese classmate and friend, Shirley Mun, as a cadaver. She recognized her due to her curly and long eyelashes. And standing beside the cadaver was Shirley's ghost.

It was then that Bubbly began seeing greenghosts for the rest of her life.

Starless Taunggyi Night

Ne Win, the dictator, closed all the universities for four months. There had been, and continue to be, violence all over Burma. Many students joined resistance groups. Many disappeared.

Bubbly is back home from Rangoon. In her room, separated by the living area where I am reading a comic book borrowed from the school library, I hear her talking to Satya and Happy about the underground student activism that they are part of at Rangoon University. I think of how positive and fun Bubbly used to be, and wonder at the new look in her eyes, eyes turned inward, steely, and resolute.

Shamsher, as we eat together in the kitchen at the low round teak wood table, averts his eyes when Bubbly speaks about the demonstration. Joth says, patting Bubbly's hand, *I am proud of you for taking part in the demonstration, but I am so glad you are home safe, Bubbly. What the army did to the student demonstrators was terrible! And unforgivable!* Then he looks at Shamsher who stares steadily at him, chewing his roti slowly. *And I hope they do not come to Taunggyi to nationalize our shops and our schools. We will become poor overnight—again.* There have been rumors. Shamsher warns us, the younger ones sitting at the table, about the military. He says: *they can crush your spirits.* Bubbly, looking directly at Shamsher, narrowing her dark eyes fringed by curling lashes, her round face stoic, says, *or they can make you stronger, bolder, and a leader. Fear itself can act like a prisoner, so to be free, we will have to let go of fear.* I look at her beautiful eyes and calm face but hear the steel behind her voice. Shamsher, who is in the middle of taking another bite from his roti and chicken curry, drops the bite on the metal plate, gets up, hurriedly washes his hands at the outdoor tap, and walks out into the dark starless Taunggyi night.

III. *Qisse* and *Kahaniyan*

You and I: Interconnected beyond the Mountains

You sit on the sun warmed ground, your long white hair newly washed and spread around you like gossamer veils. Your dark-skinned face with its deep-set eyes reassures me even after decades apart. When you disappear, when I close my eyes, when I reach out to touch you, how do you know to come back? The smell of Punjab rains, the mustard fields, your cow Janki, the newly churned butter, the carnival in the village—when was I there? Generations have gone by, but you continue to plow the fields and weave fabric of colorful *phulkari* for my half Korean granddaughter by the beach on the Pacific Ocean—ever knowing and *generative*.

Fig. 29: Laaj Kaur with cousin, Kuldeep Singh on the left of the frame and the author, Jaspal Kaur Singh, on the right in her arms, circa 1951

Singh Sisters: Fragmented

Our worlds were changing and clashing: the worlds of traditional homes of our mother *and* the liberal education and liberty as promised by the nuns and teachers at the Convent School. The Singh sisters, always playful, energetic and trail blazers, the first Indian girls to don trousers, the first ones to dance with boys to western music, the first to play badminton in co-ed sessions, the first to be beaten senseless by our authoritarian uncle with a thick teakwood stick were *also* the first of the Indian girls in Taunggyi used as examples of the educated new women.

In Taunggyi, we would ride bikes around town, our long ponytailed hair flying in the wind, and then, somedays, we would steal our father's Lambretta scooter and take off on the main road, unsteady and unstable, but resolute. Many a times one of us was found in the ditch to be rescued by father's colleagues or neighbors, but the Burmese were tolerant and amused at our antics.

The Convent School taught us ideas about liberation in modern terms. Our world was shifting.

We sisters were both sugar *and* chili, balm and sting, roses and orchids, peacocks and chimpanzees, and valleys and Rocky Mountains to each other. Sometimes we viewed each other as peace in wartime, or a harbor in a hurricane, and we became the excitement and pain of loving too much due to torturous betrayals in troubled diasporic spaces.

The journey to India and then America ripped us sisters apart. Like dried peapods, we scattered, shredding the last resolve of us sisters to love each other forever.

The Bellmaker's Daughter (A Lesson Learned on my Nani's Lap)

Nani Bishan's Bellmaker's daughter lived in Punjab: her body, her sacrifice, her voice—the sound of bells in mustard fields of Punjab, surrounded by the smell of melting metals in a cauldron, the voice of the bellmaker's daughter's trilling song heard through a stillness and silence. But why does the quietness speak to me through generations in languages difficult, but not impossible, to decipher?

The bellmaker made the sweetest sounding bells in the world. They rang like deep pools of water, echoing, and a water that was metal which celebrated the air. This bell-maker was envied by many people in the ancient Kingdom of Ram and Sita for his far-reaching melodies that caught people by surprise. His bells were distinguishable from all the other bells that hung in our village. Naturally, such a sweet creator of tintinnabulation had to have a beautiful daughter—her name was Talli.

One day the king passed by the Bellmaker's house and told him to produce the sweetest sounding bell he could from his cast metal for his kingdom. It was in the molten mixing bowls he added special ingredients: twigs from the banyan trees and pipal leaves ground to a pulp; the hair from a dark-eyed woman with the most enchanting voice, hair he burnt before adding it to the molten metal; a strip of silk from a wedding sari. The sound from the bell must be loud enough for the king's subjects to hear, but should also be sweet and mellow, like that of a koel bird. Like a sweet but strong voice that could summon the strongest of men from their most desired pleasures, bid them to come even from their wife's bed or from a scrumptious meal. But the king had a condition: the metal must be struck into the sweetest of bells or he would have the bellmaker beheaded.

The bellmaker pondered what recipe he would use this time for a bell. He wrung his hands like small bells, the knuckles cracked their tiny metal bones, and he thought about adding gold dust, but he was a poor man who only delighted in the sounds his bells made. He considered a *garuda's* wings, maybe a feather, but *garudas* were mythical creatures. Then his gaze fell upon the thirteen-year-old Talli's eyes who had wandered into the shed, the darkness of her gaze, the glowing brownness of her shoulders, her tiny, pointed breasts draped by a modest muslin fabric perky as she sniffed the silk strip. It was hot in there by the fire. When he began sorting out recipes and myths, running his calloused palm across a sheet with bee's wings, whole butterflies in splendid colors, he knew there was nothing here that would alter the cast metal into a honeyed chime. He imagines her muslin sari clinging to her moist and sweaty young body.

He slept that night without knowing what he would do. He didn't tell his wife why he stared at the bamboo roof of their hut, got up in the middle of the night and read about different metals. When he returned to bed, his wife reached out to touch him, her fingers curling around his flaccid manhood, but he turned away, his gaze turned inward, hearing a song, a voice, seeing a sweet and perfect young body. When he woke up in the morning, he thought he had only one thing to do. Did he walk into his daughter's bedroom? See her sleeping almost naked in the summer heat, her brown, supple tits staring up at him? Her neck with its youthful folds could easily be slit while she slept so innocently but sensually, her long fingers cradling one cheekbone. As he looked down at his daughter and imagine her the beautiful woman she would grow into later and a wife of a worthy man, he began to weep silently. His head fell forward into his hands. His hot tears of anguish, accompanied by his silent sobs, fell on his gnarled fingers.

The bellmaker walked away, expecting death that morning. But his daughter had not been asleep. Talli, the most desirable of girls, knew what she had to do for her father. In his metal workshop that morning, he desperately sought the key ingredients that could be cast into a belly of noise. His wife, who came into the room, set her one small gold ring by his feet. Without looking at her, he melted it and added it to the molten metal. He went out looking for more twigs from the sandalwood tree, maybe just a few more. His wife walked behind him with her little homemade cloth bag, fear for her daughter lurking in the innermost chamber of her heart, but she knew and had learned silence.

> *Talli went to the river for a morning bath. She massaged coconut oil on her body and hair. She used jasmine soap to wash her skin. When she returned home, she took off her wet muslin sari and stepped naked, her belly shimmering with oil, her long, dark hair covering her bare round buttocks, her small breasts glimmering in the light of the fire and silently jumped into the crucible containing the molten metal.*

Love and Marriage, Amritsar-Style

The Past: Still Present

I never knew that Raj, a tall, muscular turbaned Sikh man, a professor, used to be married before, but it is only when he falls in love with Jaswant, my mother's cousin, a married woman with a daughter, that their story, whispered in the domestic spaces late at night, became notorious in our family.

Ma and Jaswant or Jassi, as everyone at home called her, had reunited in 1946 Punjab when my family was displaced due to the Japanese war in Burma. Tej, still in her late teens, a young mother, had been so impressed with Jaswant, also a young mother, but who had a college education and had such progressive ideas. She got her education in Amritsar, my Nani's birthplace. It was when Jaswant came to visit Tej and her family in Peeyan that she showed Ma Raj's photo. In the photo, he indeed looked impressive, surrounded by his students, his eyes deep with an immaculately tied turban and Gandhi-style round eyeglasses. Jaswant, sharing her excitement with Tej about Amrita Preetam and about Gurbaksh Singh's progressive journal, *Preet Lari*, which Tej confided in her that she used to read as a young girl in Taunggyi, also shared her *quissa* at meeting a Gurbaksh Singh's disciple in real life:

At school, I met many liberal Sikhs who are excited about the change going on in India, and particularly, in Punjab with the Quit Indian Movement, which Raj and I are part of. There are so many factories, new roads and houses, and work for all of us, both men and women. Many Punjabi women are working outside their homes. In my school, we teachers discuss politics, education, and women's rights and arranged vs. love marriage. The last topic always lasted the longest, as we would bring up the name of the well-known writer, Gurbaksh Singh, his ideas of love in his many publications, and particularly in his monthly journal, Preet Lari where he shared his philosophy of life, ideas of western thought and modernity, and love, as you well know. He was not only famous in India, but in Burma, as you tell me, and many parts of the world as well. The one who always stood out for me with his fiery rhetoric and handsome demeanor was Raj, tall and towering, his dark blue turban immaculately tied, his voice strong as he gazed at the women in the audience of teachers, and always seem to pick me out, as I would be eating his every word. I want freedom, love, and above all else, I want to be modern.

Tejo, his looks are full of promise and passion like the ginger tea with jaggery that we consume in the school canteen or like the smell of the sugar fields on our walks during lunch times, fragrant and fecund. Life became sweet and pungent at the same time. Raj confessed to me that he was impressed with me because I am so modern. And to me, Raj looks like he could conquer the world, or my world, but, believe me, Tej, we kept to the boundaries as married individuals.

Tej, who couldn't dream of hearing such words in Burma, felt that Jaswant was like the writer and poet, Amrita Preetam, so progressive. She remembered seeing Gurmat and Jaswant's wedding photo when her aunt had written to her in Burma about their marriage. She couldn't believe that Gurmat took his own life by jumping off a running train, or so everyone in his hometown said—Gurmat, who used to be gone all day, exhausted from the train travel and from his job at the cloth factory where the supervisor used to harass the workers all day to produce more for their colonial masters.

Before they parted, as the Partition riots in Punjab became intensified, Tej had tentatively asked Jassi what actually happened to Gurmat, as she couldn't get him out of her mind, and all she said was: "He simply disappeared."

The Present: Still the Past

Decades later, I am visiting London for a conference and Ma calls me from the US to tell me to check up on Jaswant, who lives in Hayes with Raj. Jaswant's daughter Param, a cheerful, pleasant and fun-loving woman, is settled in North Carolina with her husband and daughter. We've become close and have taken a few family holidays together. I know that Jaswant is fine, but that she was having a hard time with Raj, as he has been unwell. And here we are with Jaswant driving me and the cantankerous Raj around London. She looks well, although stressed, and he, still tall and imposing, looks ravaged. As she drives the car, Raj hollers at her to be careful, to go slow or fast, to park on this or that parking spot, to repark the car, as he feels she is too near or too far off the curb. Her lips tight, her eyes glinting, she does as he says.

After the temple, Raj and Jaswant take me to the pub to eat. Raj says, "We go to the pub every Sunday." He orders beer, steak and kidney pie. She orders fish and chips. I order a beer. And some fish and chips. I eat my food with gusto and drink the beer wish relish but note that Aunty Jaswant simply nibbles at her food. Raj, who speaks non-stop on Punjab politics and famous Punjabi writers he used to hobnob with, finishes his whole meal along with a few glasses of beer. I tell them I am writing a book on Sikh writers. Jaswant, her expression softening, says, "Tej loves Amrita Pritam and Gurbaksh Singh's novels and essays. You look exactly like her when she was pregnant with Satya in Peeyan. I miss her so." Looking at Jaswant sitting across from him, Raj, who looks sort of put off at the turn of the conversion, says, "Jassi is not interested in politics or literature. All she cares is for God and for watching the kirtans on TV," and guffaws at his own words. She takes more than half of her food back home.

We sit and watch TV in their cluttered living room. She changes the channel to the Amritsar Gurudwara where Sikh hymns are live streamed all day long from the Golden Temple. She covers her head, bows to the TV which is covered with a white crocheted tablecloth. Raj, who had a few more beers since we got home, says in a slurry voice, "Jassi, warm me some milk." As she leaves for the kitchen, she summons me with her eyes to follow her.

Palo, where shall I begin? It is all my fault. Love is a myth.

You are like Tej to me. Let me tell you something about Raj that I used to share with her. He used to be so handsome and proud, a wonderful teacher, a head and shoulder above the other man in Amritsar, believing in love and free choice for both men and women, gender equality for Independent India, and dared to divorce his wife and marry me, a widow with a young daughter, dared to migrate to England with us, and I wonders what my fate might have been if I had remained unmarried and not fallen for this once devilishly handsome man—but let me tell you something more—here he is now, rotten to the core, ordering me around as if I were his maid, sitting and reading his endless newspapers. I will ask God when I'm dead if this is what is called justice—is it because you are male, God? Why do I still believe in you? Is it because you recused me from the life of an Indian widow whose daughter would surely have been taken advantage of by the males in the family and community due to the shame I brought to them? What could I have done, a fallen woman, called spoilt by my family, when things turned sour for me in London? Where could I go with my daughter when I barely knew anyone in England? God, you will surely forgive me for putting up with him when he . . . when he . . . But what could he do, she was so alluring, so beautiful, so young and so helpless? What could I do, as I had to work for a living to feed him and my daughter, as he lost his job after his accident? If I had left him or to leave him now, this time around not only my family and community, but the whole world would judge me, once in love with a married man, once widowed, then married to a divorced man, so what choice do I really have?

Present and Past: ambiguous times

Two years later, my cousin Param calls me to tell me that her mother is dead at eighty-two. Apparently, one evening, as Raj and Jaswant finished watching the kirtan program being live streamed from the Amritsar Golden Temple, Jaswant got up to cover the TV for the night, bowed her head, and slumped to the floor, never to get up to serve God or Raj again. Param had returned to London, took care of Jaswant's funeral, sold the house in Hayes, and took her stepfather back home to the US to live with her. She says she wants to forgive and forget, maybe put the London past to rest.

After her return to the US, she calls me after a few months, "Palo, every day, I cook for him and take him to the doctor for checkups. I bought him new clothes and shoes. Decorated his room with new furniture, his bed with new bedcovers and pillows. My daughter dotes on the old man. She hugs and kisses him. My granddaughter, a three-year-old, sits snugly in his lap. He kisses and fondles her. I hold my tongue and anger, Palo." She knows her mother's testimony to me, I think. I say to her, "What do you want, Param?" She remains silent. Then, she says, "He never once asked for forgiveness."

Param places him in a nursing home after he falls sick one year later. When I call her, she tells me, "He is so weak, and I had to get help. He doesn't like the nursing home. He asked for a cell phone. He constantly calls me, demanding special food, medicine and his beloved magazines. He has become so abusive. Of course, I am upset, unsure if I could ever forgive or forget his abuses, but I want to. And I had promised mother to keep my peace."

Last Traces of the Past

Param's Qissa: I was running around, completing my work duties, quickly filing away the papers my boss left, aiming to complete the work on time, so I could run home to cook before going to check on Papaji. Frantic with the rush to complete my work, I finally had a moment to check my phone and saw that Papaji had called. Putting the last file in place, I drove to the Nursing home. As I reached his room, I saw him lying on his back, his large eyes staring accusingly at me. "Param, where the hell have you been? Didn't you see I have been calling you forever?" "Papaji," I asked, "'What do you need?" I looked at him, lying defenselessly there in a pile of grey sheets. *How could he have intimidated me all these years ago? How could he have abused and violated my body and my soul for so long when I was so young and new in London?*

He looks like a rag doll. Glaring at me with his bulging eyes, he said, "I have been waiting for you for a long time. A long time. Come closer." As I reached his bed, he motioned me to his feet. Unsure what he wanted, I hesitated. He cried, "Get my damn shoes off! I have been waiting for a long time for you!" I bent my aching back, undid the laces of his white shoes and took them off his feet. I heard him sigh."

Param tells me that when she lifted her head with a regretful look, she saw a half smile lingering on his still fleshy lips. "He was dead."

Mandalay Prison

After the Burmese military regime nationalized all the businesses (our family shop and schools included) after the 1962 coup, all the shops were renamed "People's Shop," and we had to wait in long lines for our daily ration. As we were a joint family of eleven children (six siblings and five cousins), parents, grandmother, three uncles, one married, we were all recruited by our father to stand in line for food.

Cousin Kul and I, both of us barely ten-years old, would stand in line for hours, feeling scared of the men in military uniforms with their long rifles and stern faces. Father went to the Five-Day Market and rented a stall. It was built of bamboo and had rattan floor. He began selling handloomed *longyis* from the Inlay Lake region. He also bought colorful Chinese towels and bedsheets. One day, my brother Happy, who was just twelve years old, was asked to go on a bike to the Five-Day Market with a packet. My uncle Saran followed him a few paces behind. My father took the packet, rolled it in a towel, and a few minutes later, handed it to a well-dressed Shan man. When my brother told me the story in the evening, I asked what was in the packet. He said, "Imported watches." Kul and I came home with the grocery along with a few apples wrapped in a gauzy material. We'd never eaten apples before. They were fragrant and looked just like the pictures from our school English Reader. The next day, Uncle Saran was arrested and sent to the dreaded Mandalay prison where he had to do hard labor.

Fig. 30: Mother, Tej Kaur with Manjit on the right side of the fame with Prab Joth behind her and Uncle Saran on the left side of the frame, posing for an ID photo which must be mounted in the entrance of the home after the military coup in Burma, circa 1970

1975: Ajeet and Ko Hla, A Burmese Love Story

The small Sikh community in Taunggyi is varied with some professionals but mostly traders and service people serving the predominantly Shan and Burmese communities. Traditions are strictly followed or imposed. Marriages, arranged by parents, are celebrated at the Sikh Temple on the main road. Henna and dance ceremonies are held at the bride or groom's homes and almost all (except for the low caste and the working-class Sikhs) are invited. Ajeet and Ko Hla's marriage, however, was not celebrated at the temple or in the homes because it was interracial.

Ajeet or Jeeti, a qualified nurse, was transferred to a remote Burmese village. Her older sister, Balbir or Balli, an English schoolteacher still lived at home, unmarried at 28, not for lack of suitors, but because no one was good enough for his daughters as far as their father Amar was concerned.

Ajeet's *quissa, told in her own words, translated:*

One day, a patient, a Danu Shan farmer, was gored by a bull and was admitted to the hospital. The wound was on his behind. Jeeti had to be very careful. After all, it was a delicate matter. As soon as she finished dressing his wounds, he asked, "What's your name?"

"Ajeet."

"What does your name mean?"

"Victorious One."

"Are you married?"

Ajeet shook her head but tried to keep her professional demeanor and jabbed his arm with the needle.

"*Amaleh!* That hurts," he said, but his eyes were smiling.

His boldness took her by surprise, but something within her answered to his boldness, and she gave him the benefit of her full smile.

"My name is Ko Hla," he said.

Ko Hla, the beautiful one, and yes, she thought, what a beautiful man, so calm and placid, a Buddhist.

Jeeti thought about him all evening, gazing into the distant green rice fields, her eyes narrowing against the evening sun. She sighed. Life. She knew she would never see him again. And rightly so.

But the day after he was discharged, he came back and said without preamble, looking straight into her warm brown eyes, "Ajeet, now I am no longer your patient, I have come to ask if you like me as much as I like you."

Her heart constricted. Joy and fear struggled within her. Oh, the potentials and the consequences. Lifetimes are changed in moments. Future generations are imagined and celebrated. Or imagined and abandoned.

She knew she could never say yes to Ko Hla. Her father would kill her. Jeeti's eyelids fluttered, becoming heavy.

"Ko Hla, I am a Sikh, and you are Shan, a Buddhist. We shouldn't."

Her blood swirled in the pit of her stomach, and she felt queasy. What was she saying? She would never meet anyone like him ever again. Oh, the rules of the mundane world!

"Ko Hla, please understand. My parents would either die or kill us if I did anything against their wishes."

"Ajeet, all I ask is a chance to show you how much I care. You will never want for anything in this lifetime if you say yes." She watched his retreating back and unbowed dark head, and heard her own words echoing in the evening breeze, "no . . ."

Slow days passed and then months. Her eyes scanned the fields, and the path beside it, hoping to see a familiar figure walk towards her bamboo hut.

One day, at the five-day bazaar, Ko Hla, along with Daw Sein, his mother, who had a basket full of green and yellow vegetables, stopped in front of Jeeti as she was selecting a fresh caught fish. Their hands reached for the same fish. Daw Sein smiled, and handed the fish to her, while Ko Hla, who was a step behind his mother, with smiling but anxious eyes, said, "Mingala ba, Ajeet." After the introductions, they decided to have mashed fish rice and green tea at the open-air stall under the banyan tree. Jeeti handed Daw Sein the fish, saying, "Can you share your recipe for the fish"? Daw Sein felt the undercurrents of emotions immediately. She knew what she had to do to help fate along. Her smile, as she looked at Jeeti, was tender and loving.

Jeeti remembered how her community in Taunggyi would look at her with a mixture of pity and distaste whenever she told them she was Amar and Preet Kaur's daughter, Preet Kaur of the dark visage. That he was a drunk and an abusive alcoholic father no one cared about. Or did they?

And here were Daw Sein and Ko Hla, looking at her so affectionately and kindheartedly. With an unknown sadness in her heart, bowing her head in respect to Daw Sein, looking down at her feet, and unable to meet Ko Hla's eyes, she picked up a freshly fallen banyan leaf, saying, "I wonder how many ghosts live on this tree?" Daw Sein, as Ko Hla and she were taking their leave of Jeeti after their tea, said, almost with anticipation and hope, "How beautiful you are, *tami*," calling her daughter, touching Jeeti's bowed head as a blessing. "I will see you again soon." *Hope*, Jeeti thinks, *a thing or creature I have no familiarly with*, but somehow, she imagined reaching out to touch the fleeting thing with tentative and expectant fingers.

Oh, but Ko Hla! He was patient. Six months later, he turned up at Jeeti's house that stood at the corner of the only street in the village. When she came home from work, she found him sitting, legs folded in a lotus position on the bamboo floor outside her huts, with bowed head and folded hands, respectfully saying, "I beseech you to reconsider my proposal." His face has the timeless look of the Shan people, born of the mountains, patient and solid as the oak, but oh so tender like the young bamboo plants!

You see, there is a Burmese, and particularly a Danu-Shan, tradition. When a man loves you and you too love him, and he comes to your house, sits down with respect, and asks to marry you, and even if no one else agrees, but you do, you become husband and wife. Then your marriage is sanctioned by the community.

She meditated for two full days: her heart full of trepidation. On the third day, she saw a bluish light deep within her, and she calmly and serenely reached out to touch Ko Hla's hands with her left hand while wrapping the warm fingers of her right hand around his face. She felt cocooned in his warmth and ardor. They were married the next day according to Shan rites. Jeeti looked beautiful in her top knot, decorated with Jasmine blossoms, and her wedding outfit of purple embroidered silken *longyi* and *ingi*. Ko Hla, his arms, legs, and torso tattooed in red, black and purple in the manner of the Shans, covered his body with loose earth-brown cotton pants and shirt along with a *taik pong*—a high collared Shan Jacket, and a *gaung paung*—traditional head gear. He sat motionless, holding back his heart's pleasure, looking at his lovely bride, Ajeet, Victorious One, as his dark, slanted eyes sparkled with thousands of mindful joys, and feeling blissful, he gave thanks to his ancestors and to Buddha.

Over one hundred Buddhist monks were fed.

The *kong-kong-kongo-kong* of the Shan drums and the *tring tring* of Burmese *Saung Kauk* reverberated into the mountains, the farming community ate their fill of the pork roast curry and Shan rice, black rice pudding, and fried plantains and everyone danced late into night around the log fire.

Days and nights merged with the rhythm of the warm seasons of the Shan States, as the newlyweds' lifeforces intertwined in pleasurable activities, making love under the mosquito net, drinking black *laphet yei* in early dawn, eating *Kaungipaung* and *Peybyoke* for breakfast, going off to work, she to the clinic and he to the fields, joyously reuniting in the late afternoon to sit on the veranda, drink *laphet yei* and eat some *laphet tot*, planning and cooking dinner together in their sparsely furnished bamboo home. Jeeti told Ko Hla, "I never knew such happiness existed." He simply said, "*Jeeti yei, thait chit tai naw*" his eyes, every smiling, serious for a moment, as he quietly thanked their ancestors and the *nats* for keeping them and their love safe.

A year later, Jeeti was pregnant with Mon To. As the child stirred in her womb, she got a message from her sister in Taunggyi that her mother was very ill and was asking to see her. When she told Ko Hla, he said, "Ajeet, you must go immediately. Your mother needs you." He knew about her mother's situation and her fate with Amar. That evening, he stood at the bus station long after the bus was gone with his wife and their unborn child, feeling an unknown emotion . . . no, not fear, but some other form of trepidation, a trepidation born of the unknown, of differences and cultures, of some idea of what it might mean to be an outcast or a stranger amongst one's own family and illusory community.

Jeeti had barely stepped foot in the house when Amar dragged her and locked her up in his room.

"Please let me out. I am with child, Ko Hla's child. Please!"

Her cries were in vain.

After a week of being locked up, her father, eyes red and short hair disheveled, came into the room.

"Listen Jeeti, I am ready to overlook all your misdeeds. I have talked to a number of people from the Sikh Temple. Surat Singh is willing to marry you. He knows you are with child. He doesn't mind."

Jeeti couldn't believe that her father would consider the penniless Surat Singh, a *Ka Bya*, a biracial man, half Burmese and half Sikh, but would have nothing to do with a perfectly respectable Shan man!

"Do what you want, Papaji, I will not marry Surat Singh. I am Ko Hla's wife. I love him."

"Love! What do you know about love, you ungrateful *kanjari*! I love you, what about that? I will teach you what love is."

His fingerprints on her face and body turned blue the next day.

Their Burmese neighbor's wife whispered to Jeeti, as she stood by the window with iron grills barring her escape, that Ko Hla, disguised as a *Palaung mountain* man with an elaborate colorful headgear was seen walking past toward the steps of the pagoda behind their house, always looking, looking towards her window.

Chindo, helpless at her daughter's plight, stole into her room a few times, hugging her and crying bitter tears, saying, "Why, Jeeti, why did you invite such violence into your life? You know him. He will break your bones. It is our fate" Jeeti looked at her broken mother, small and dark, with such big brown eyes, who is unwilling or unable to see the truth, the truth about love and hate, about hope and violence, about invitation and force, about choice and fate, and hugged her close to her heart and cried for them all, but she knew another truth, another reality, another love. She must escape.

One night, her mother, Chindo, inadvertently, or so it appeared to her family, left the back door of the house open while she went to fetch coal from the shed behind the house, as the nights were getting cold. Jeeti took the opportunity to slip out into the cold, dark night. She ran barefooted all the way to Ko Hla's relative's home near the pagoda. He had a jeep ready. They left Taunggyi that very night and didn't return for a long, long time.

Idyllic years followed Ko Hla and Jeeti. Their son, Mon To, who looked like Jeeti with her round, brown eyes, was almost two. She also continued to work as a nurse at the district hospital and the village clinic. Daw Sein and Mon To, seen around the fields and the village street, became inseparable. Ko Hla, who adored his son, took him along with him after work to his relatives, who spoiled him with *tha nyet*, fried *khao pok* or *Tofu*. Jeeti adored Mon To's speech, a mixture of Shan and Pa'O, with a sprinkling of Punjabi, which she found so endearing!

Motherhood, Jeeti realized, was a blessing. She also realized that her love for her child was all encompassing. Therefore, when she was pregnant with her second child, her thoughts turned again towards Chindo, her mother.

Balli wrote her a letter, letters which were few and far between. Chindo was very sick again. As Ko Hla, whose arms and legs were covered in mud, as it was rice planting season, came in from the fields, Jeeti said, her eyes full of sorrow, "Mother is very sick again."

He started packing their bags without a word. They rode the bus all day long, and as they saw the mountains silhouetted against the starry night, he sighed. "Ajeet, your Cherry land is here."

When they entered her parents' wooden house, Chindo, black eyes staring out from her small face, hair in a tight thin braid hanging by the side of her head, sobbed uncontrollably at the sight of Mon To who she was seeing for the first time, "Jeeti, my daughter; Mon To, my love, you came after all!"

She sat with her mother, who continued to cradle Mon To, for hours.

"Mon To. Who am I?"

"*Nani*"

Ko Hla sat by Chindo and massaged her feet while Jeeti pressed her forehead. Amar was absent, having gone out of town to visit his friends in Rangoon.

On that trip, Jeeti left her first born with them as a peace offering, crying all the way back home. Ko Hla, heart split like a ripe tomato, held her hand, soothing her, saying, "He is with his Nani, his *Ahmayji*, big mother." It took Mon To months before he stopped crying and for Bally to understand his words. Then, one day, he turned to Balli, who had been trying to sooth the crying boy with toys and books for days, and started calling her *Ah May*, Mother.

In the mundane world, Samsara, whenever a tyrant is born, so is a redeemer and a reformer. The situation in Burma worsened under the military rule. Ko Hla became part of the militia, helping protect the villages from both the army and the Shan separatists. The so-called insurgents looted the villages, and the army did the same and, in fact, did nothing to protect the innocent people. Ko Hla rode a horse, armed, and patrolled the villages. Soon both the insurgents and the army became frustrated, needing food and arms.

The Shan hills were green, and the monsoon rain was falling in torrents. The fields were fecund and the trees laden. Jeeti and Ko Hla, who were blessed again with a child, Win Win, a sweet daughter who was the apple of her father's eyes, a splitting image of his mother, became enmeshed in the rhythm of the season again even though there was a hole in their hearts the size of Mon To. Bally wrote how well-adjusted and loving Mon To was and how much Amar doted on his grandson. Amar had asked Bally to write and invite Ko Hla and Jeeti, and particularly Win Win, his granddaughter, to visit during the Tazaungdaing festival, which was in a few months. Jeeti trembled in Ko Hla's arms that night, as he soothed her with whispered words, "Our ancestors are blessing us, Ajeet, my Victorious one!"

The next few months were brutal for the Shan State Army and for the villagers. The Burmese army mounted one of its most violent largescale attacks on them. Although the opium smuggling in the Golden Triangle, which the Shan States was part of, flourished, people were starving and fighting for scraps in the rural areas. Thousands became refugees on the Thai-Burma border.

One evening, a month before Tazaungdaing, in the still of the Shan twilight, the boy next door came running to their house.

"Father wishes to see Uncle Hla."

Ko Hla, who had just finished feeding Win Win, his little daughter, turned to leave.

"Please take your rifle."

"Oh, Ajeet *yai*, I am only going to Uncle's house."

After about fifteen minutes, Jeeti heard six gun shots. She looked up from stirring the stir-fried squash, the crows, returning home at sunset to settle on the padauk tree, screeched and scattered, but she was used to hearing shots as the People's Army practiced almost every evening. When eight members of the People's Army came up to her house, their faces grim, she couldn't get up. She felt her third child contort in her womb.

Fig. 31: Ajeet Kaur, circa 1965

Fig. 32: Ajeet Kaur, circa 1959

Fig. 33: Ko Hla and Ajeet, circa 1972

Memories of 1962: Burma

1962 Burma. Ne Win's military coup toppled the democratically elected government. Nationalization began in earnest: Banks, businesses, schools, universities in major cities. The city of Taunggyi in the Shan States waited for the army. Some thought the Shan States would be spared. My father certainly did. His shop was chock full of merchandize that he had, just before the coup, restocked from his buying trip to Rangoon. He worried about my sister studying at the university of Rangoon. Protesting students had been murdered by the military and rumors abounded of shallow graves by the Irrawaddy River. Our school, St. Anne's Convent, was still operating, but we heard whispers of nationalization in the Shan States as well. What will the Irish and Italian nuns do if that happened? Would they be deported? I was in the third grade that summer. I went to father and asked him for a leather belt for my convent school uniform. We all wore loose box-pleated navy-blue tunics and white long-sleeved shirts. We needed belts if we didn't want to look pregnant. He said: *I will give it to you after the summer break.*

Early in the morning before the sun rose over the Taunggyi mountains a few days later, army tanks rolled into the town. The Main Road, where most of the businesses were located, was overtaken by the military. As father went to open his general store, a shop across the street from the Sikh Gurudwara, army officers followed him in. Holding back tears and fear, he handed over his keys to the shop and the keys to his cash register. After he showed them the books, he was asked to leave. His shop, which he and his brother had worked so hard to transform from the tin shack into this concrete and glass affair after their displacement due to the Partition, was now the People's Shop # so and so. When Joth reached home, he told Tej, my mother, his bearded and turbaned face ashen: *We lost everything.* Mother, also turning pale, her small frame shrinking further, reaches out to put her hands soothingly on his back. "I have some gold jewelry. We could pawn it in the market." I silently followed father and mother up the back stairs of our house. I never got the belt, but then, my school was nationalized, and I had to wear ethnic Burmese clothes, a blue *longyi* and white *inji*, to school: I didn't need the belt, anyway.

Fig. 34: Jaspal Kaur Singh, last row, 2nd on the right, with schoolmates, circa 1966, four years after the military coup in Burma

Punjab is Burning: Surviving Genocide (Stories I heard from my family in 1984)

Diljeet Kaur raises the Kalashnikov to her shoulder and fires.

"I think he is dead."

Flexed fingers release bruised petals. One by one, the ragtag army of the Khalistan Liberation Front comes into view.

The campfire helps warm them in the cool night.

The nightly ritual begins.

Surjit Kaur tells her tale without preamble.

"We were naked. In Delhi's model town. The Hindu mob grabbed us, tore off our salwar kameez, and raped us in front of Beyji and Pitaji. They then grabbed Pitaji and Jaswant, my brother, took off their turbans, jammed car tires around their necks, cut off their long hair, poured kerosene on them, and set their bodies on fire."

Her eyes are flat riverbeds.

Jaspal Kaur raises her Kalashnikov: "*Boley So Nihal!*" and starts speaking:

"In Dehradun. In Karanpur Bazaar. The mob came to our house. Dragged us out to the streets. Stripped us naked. Raped me and my sister. My sister joined the KLF. Died in custody."

Her face is a moonscape.

And night, slowly darkening, dances to dholak drumbeat. Women dance the *giddha*, the dance of the new harvest. Tall strong Punjabi men in colorful turbans stamp their feet and dance the *bhangra*.

Punjab is ablaze.

III. aromas and colors of home

The Transforming Story of Tea

Shenong, the Divine Farmer and the father of Chinese agriculture, was boiling water when small, elongated dried Camellia leaves from the delicate stems of a bush blew and landed in the water, infusing it with a light smoky fragrance. Tea, then, was discovered. After cultivating and learning the mystery of this plant, he imparted knowledge about tea cultivation and its use to others. One must, he said, harvest and dry them on the third day of the third month for best therapeutic results. In ancient times, Chinese people mixed salt, oil, and cooked or dried fish to the steamed tealeaves liquid, as snacks for they believed it provided energy. Used in religious rituals and in medicinal forms for headaches and stomach ailments, tea drinking only became a social custom in the Tang Dynasty (618-907). Raised by Buddhist monks, Lu Yu (715-803) wrote *Ch'a Ching* or the *The Book of Tea* or *Classics of Tea* in which he explains the fine technique of tea growing, cultivation, preparing and serving this "dew of heaven" he called *cha*.

"Goodness is a decision for the mouth to make," said Lu Yu. And now millions of mouths have attested to the goodness of tea, including the taste of the inexpressible Burmese *laphet tot.*

Saicho, Zen Buddhist Monk and Tea Infusions

It is said: Saicho, a Zen Buddhist monk studying in China, woke up one morning to the smell of tea wafting over the small wooden hut that he slept in after his meditations. He could stay calm with one infusion and with another he could stay alert, so during long meditations, he used the latter while during his free periods, he used the former. He particularly liked the first when he felt homesick for Japan, the sight of Mount Fuji, the sound of Japanese language. Thus, was he exposed to the "Dew of Heaven" or *cha* in the 9th Century. Upon returning home to Japan, he shared the tea brought from China in brick form with the other monks. The brick, warmed over flames, was shaved off bit by bit, boiled in hot water, and served in a china bowl. Emperor Saga, the 52nd emperor of Japan, finally encouraged and saw to the cultivation of tea around the Kyoto region. However, it was a few centuries later after Eisai, the founder of the Rinzai sect of Zen Buddhism (1141-1215) who brought back tea plants from Sung China, that tea became popular among mainstream Japanese. Once it did, however, tea preparation and service developed into an addition to Zen philosophy's ritualized pureness. Japanese tea ceremony, *chanoyu*—where each movement of serving tea requires skills, such as gracefulness and sitting still in meditative poses—uses leaves from bushes that are grown in the shade for the last few weeks before the harvest, whose leaves are ground in a mortar and pestle into a fine power, called matcha. At the tea ceremony, the guests remove their shoes at the door. They then sit on the floor. The server bows to the drinkers, wipes the bowl, and serves the tea carefully and meditatively to the guests. In this way, a community is created, a community of shared language and taste that Saicho longed for when he had felt adrift in the strange waters of China. Home, to the monk, was a place of grace and patience that dwells in the shade of the mighty Mount Fuji—with a shared heavenly smell and language.

Ramayana and Tea Drinking in India

In 750 to 500 BC, tea drinking is cited in the *Ramayana*, the sacred Hindu text, but for the next thousand years or so, there is no mention of tea in written records in India. Oral history suggests its medicinal use; however, it was not until the British colonial period that tea was re-introduced into India. The British colonizers began cultivating it in large quantities as they became hooked to tea drinking and to selling it—in colonial India and in England. The states of Assam and Darjeeling were marked by the colonizers to become large producers and cultivators of tea although eventually the entire foothills of the Himalayas became strewn with the emerald tea bushes. Women in saris, *ghagra cholis* and flower printed scarves with long handled baskets looped over their heads can be seen plucking tea leaves at various times in the foothills. Picturesque. But back breaking. They get paid $1.50 for a day's worth of picking. Women make up almost 53% of the workforce in tea plantations. Many live below the poverty line in India. They still feel lucky to be tea pluckers, they say: *Otherwise, we would starve.*

Ceylonese Tea

The Island nation of Sri Lanka, previously known as Ceylon, began the cultivation of tea by default. British colonizers in 1825 meant to grow coffee which, although initially successful, was abandoned as a fungus destroyed the entire crop; so, by 1870, tea production began in the mountain regions of Kandy and Ceylon and their tea became legendary in the world due to British distributions. In 1867, James Taylor, a Scot having recently arrived in Ceylon, oversaw the first sowing of tea. His beautiful teakwood bungalow with a wraparound veranda overlooked the sea of tea bushes. He used the large veranda to dry and roll the tea by hand. These leaves were roasted over a coal fired clay oven. This tea was an instant hit with the people of the empire and was served, it is believed, to Queer Victoria, who quite relished a "cuppa" from Ceylon.

John Field, High Commissioner for Great Britain in Sri Lanka in 1992, wrote, "It can be said of very few individuals that their labors have helped to shape the landscape of a country. But the beauty of the hill country as it now appears owes much to the inspiration of James Taylor, the man who introduced tea cultivation to Sri Lanka."

When I visited Sri Lanka in 2012, I saw women of all ages in long skirts and bright shirts plucking tea and putting it in the baskets hanging behind their backs, the long handle of the basket looped around their heads—backbreaking work. At the end of the day, they get paid by the kilos. If they pluck 18 kilos, they get the equivalent of $4.00. If they pluck less than that, they get paid only $2.00.

Sri Lanka is the second largest exporter of tea. Tea pluckers, mostly landless, remain the poorest group in the Island nation.

Tea served in Tulip glasses at the Istanbul's Grand Bazaar

Although Turkey trails behind India, China, Kenya, Sri Lanka and Indonesia in tea production, the per capita consumption rate of tea by the Turks is highest in the world and averages about 1,000 cups per year for each person. Teahouses or tea gardens, where hot tea is served in small tulip glasses, became the social norms for outgoing and Europeanized Istanbulus, where traditionally, women were not allowed. It was in the 15th century that tea made its way through Turkey along the Silk Route, but it was only in the 19th century that tea drinking became popular with the local people due to its popularity in Europe through British colonialism. Today, tea is served in all social settings, in bazaars, such as the Grand Bazaar, one of the largest and oldest covered bazaars with over 3,000 shops in Istanbul or the New Mosque Spice Bazaars, or the Egyptian Spice Bazaar, the second largest in Istanbul, at bridal showers and circumcision ceremonies. Male Turks still predominantly populate most public teahouses in the contemporary period. As Turkey became modernized and secularized as a nation-state through governmental ordinances and the alphabet revolution of Mustafa Kemal Ataturk in the early 20th century, the religious and spiritual elements were relegated to the domestic spaces, the spaces of tea making. Tea is brewed in large double boiler, *caydanlik* or samovar, and served with a cube or two of sugar. In the rural areas of Turkey, during a Bridal Shower, sometimes held in Turkish hammams or baths, women prepare samovars of tea and sweets for all the guests who partake of the refreshments after their communal baths. Tassology is practiced within domestic spaces where tea leaves are often read or divined—to choose brides, to start or expend a business, to build a new house, or to get rid of malevolent djinns or invite good ones into one's life.

I saw rows upon rows of emerald tea bushes in 2012 when I was in Turkey: Hip high with small leaves, bitter when freshly cut. The bushes can be seen stretching from the mountains of the border towns of Georgia to the Black Sea Coasts. Tea processing companies, such as Cay Kur, where I tasted the tea in a tulip glass, cultivate white, black and oolong teas. Crush, Tear, Curl, or CTC methods, where leaves are passed through cylindrical rollers with sharp metal pins that splits them, are used for tea production. Tea plucking needs precision and care and tea pluckers, majority of whom are women, old and young, pluck only the top of the plant, two leaves and a bud.

Royal Shans and *Laphet* Tea

Burma produces 78 million kilos of green tea annually, but the best quality comes from the Northern Shan States (where I was born and raised) in the mountainous regions of Namhsan. The altitude ranges from 1200 to 1800 meters above sea level. *Nagar Pyan*, Flying Dragon, Company is one of the major cultivators and producers in this region. King Alaung Sitthu (AD 1113-1167) introduced tea in to the Burmese Shans. Tea was a luxury and only the royal family and the ministers used to partake of it. Within Burmese homes, green tea is kept brewing day and night, and family and visitors alike partake of it throughout the day. Generally, women and children sit around a low wooden table, the women knitting or sewing, talking about household affairs, drinking tea. Men from the family will drift in and out throughout the day, staying awhile, drinking tea or eating some *laphat* tea salad set-aside in partitioned lacquerware bowls for the men and for special guests.

Kyaukme, a small town in the Northern Shan States Mountains, became one of the major colonial hubs for tea plantation and trading. Most of the tea ends up either as green or black tea, but for the local markets, about 20% of it is fermented and sold at the five-day bazaar by the Shan people. Only Shan States has the fermented tea tradition. The Palaung people grow tea at an altitude of 6,000 feet. They place baskets of green tea underground for months for the tea to become fermented. Legend has it that two kingdoms fought bitterly over the land for decades, but once they reconciled, they sat down peacefully to eat *Lephat tot* tea salad to bury the hatchet. The reality is Shan States became part of the golden triangle for opium trade with Vietnam and Thailand during the troubled years in Burma when it was under the Ne Win's military regime and, even today, poppy plantations are increasingly more attractive to cultivate than tea; however, all Burmans are hooked to tea (and many to drugs, as my cousins and friends were, and still are) and the Shans are especially addicted to tea salad, so the cultivation, even on a smaller scale, continues in Burma.

Black Pepper and Red Chilies (heat up your life!)

Black peppers, round, grainy with pruney surface, can be used whole or in powdered form in food preparation. When black peppers are still green, they can be pickled and eaten with food. The vines twirl around a solid green tree, as it cannot support itself. Black pepper powder, universally used to flavor food, a pinch here, a few peppercorns there, is the extent of its usage in food. Red chili pepper now, what can one not do with it! First, before it turns red, it is green and hot, hot, hot. One can eat it green with mustard greens and corn *rotis*, with gobs of homemade butter, as farmers in Punjab do, or one can slice it real thin, sprinkle some salt and lime juice over it, add a few sliced red onions, and eat the lot with saffron flavored chicken biryani, or simply with plain dal and rice. One can stuff the green or red chilies with a mix of tamarind paste, dried green pomegranate seeds, some crushed cumin and coriander seeds, a teaspoon of crushed red chili powder, a bit of grated ginger and garlic, coat them with a paste of powdered *besan* (chickpea) powder, drop them in smoking hot peanut oil until golden brown, eat them with a hot cup of spiced cardamom tea, or with a glass of red wine, or my favorite, with a glass of scotch over ice—to sooth the deliciously burning tongue. When dried, the red chili could be ground into a coarse or fined powder and used in curries, pickles, dals, raita, pakoras, *kachouries*, and most savory dishes one prepares. I make a garlic chili paste from scratch that I use in almost every dish. Adding a spoonful of red chili powder to slowly frying garlic slices, I stir it over low heat until the chili powder is smoking hot, almost but not quite burnt, and then rescue it from the gas stove and immediately pour it into a glass jar. This red chili and garlic, scarlet oil floating on top, a teaspoon or two of the mix, added to Burmese tea salad, a cheese toast, rice and curry, or simply rolled into a roti and eaten with a hot cup of chai is enough to make one's mouth sing for the rest of the day, or until one is ready to think of another meal where one uses whole dried chilies to smoke up and flavor some hot oil for frying pieces of chicken with a touch of soy sauce and some peanuts to be eaten at dinner with freshly cooked basmati rice. Small red chilies—sliced, rubbed with salt, set out in the sunshine for a few hours, along with cubed or sliced green mangoes, then pickled in mustard oil with coarsely grounded coriander, fenugreek, mustard, and fennel seeds, along with finely powdered turmeric, red chili powder, salt—add not only fire to the green mangoes, but colors the glass pickle jar set out in the windowsill for a few days of seasoning in the sun. Whether the chili is small, tiny, the size of your fingernail, or big, like your whole hand, whether it is green or dried, crushed or sliced, fried or sautéed, pickled or cooked, stuffed or coated, it never fails to arouse one's taste buds, leads one to tears of joy, cries of agony, or orgasmic stupor, unlike the tame and cultured pepper, which at the best can decorate a sunny side egg, a creamed soup, or at worst, lead a cultured lady to a half suppressed polite sneeze.

Kalaaudi and *Laphet*: Tiny Green Chili Peppers and Fermented Tea Salad

The name of the small chili peppers is *kalaaudi*. It means that eating one will make even an Indian cry (or a white foreigner, but Indians like to take the credit for the naming).

Premo's (whose given name is Bachan Kaur, but all her relatives, when she lived in a little Village in Burma, used to call her Premo, so even after her marriage, when Amar also began calling her by that name, it stuck) oiled uncut hair is slicked back into a long braid on which hangs homemade cotton tassels, dyed with vegetable colors, red, yellow and green, reaching down to her waist. Squatting on a wooden stool in the half open kitchen in front of the fireplace, she picks up the *kalaaudis* in her small dark hands, slices them into tiny pieces, rubs salt into them, sets them aside. From a bottle, she takes a pile of sesame seeds. From another, a handful of peanuts. Another handful of flat beans. Some *channa* dal. Sliced fresh garlic. Whole dried red chilies. Singing her favorite Sikh hymn, *Jaati ochha, paati ochha, ochha janum hamar, Raja Ram ki sev na keeney, kahey Ravi Das chamara.* "My caste and creed are low; only through your worship and service, O Ram, will I, Ravi Das the sweeper, will find salvation." *Why does he make me feel as if I am casteless, an untouchable?* She unhooks the iron wok from a rusted hook hammered sideways into the crumbling termite infested wall, places it on the open wooden fire, and adds half a cup of peanut oil. Continuing to hum, "My caste is low, my creed is low, low is my birth," she drops the peanuts in the medium hot oil and stirs them with her wooden spatula. *My dark skin makes my birth low.* She rescues the peanuts and puts them on a tray. Then, she puts the dried flat beans in the oil, sautés, and then adds them to the peanuts. Last, she drops the sliced garlic in the hot oil, takes one burning wooden log out of the fire, and places the wok back on it. Low heat. Stir slowly. As the garlic browns, she places dried whole red chilies in the mortar and using the stone pestle, pounds them into small pieces. From a jar, she takes a tablespoon full of fine ground chili powder and mixes it in the mortar. After a final stir of the garlic, she adds both the chili mix—the fine and the coarse ground—and fries for about a minute. A pungent, piquant, and smoky earthy flavor mingles with Premo's memory of warm salty blood when Amar's backhanded slap had split open her full lower lip. She craves salty and sour foods lately. Putting her dark hand on her stomach, she thinks: *Will the flavors from her kitchen make it all the way up the mountain to the Standing Buddha? O Buddha, save this one.* Her eyelids flutter for a moment, then close. *Buddham Saranam Gacchâmi. Dhammam Saranam Gacchâmi. Sangham Saranam Gacchâmi.* She cleans the weevils in the broken rice pieces, systematically placing them between her thumb nails, crushing them, enjoying the sound, or simply throws them in the open fire. Listening to them pop, she goes back to singing the Sikh hymn under her breath, *Tum chandan hum eerind bapuray, sang turmarey baasa, neech rukh te unch bayeihai, gand sugandh niwasa.* "You are the fragrant sandal wood tree, I'm a foul-smelling castor oil vine, twined around you, I hope to become fragrant, like you."

Premo's tongue slowly licks her lip. She tastes a fermented tealeaf, *laphet*, with the peanuts and chili oil. Her swollen lower lip burns.

The Danu Shan, the Burmese Tamadaw and The Shan States Independence Armies

Burma became an independent and a democratic nation-state in 1948 after a brutal colonial regime, but many ethic people were unhappy with the divisions. When General Ne Win wrests power from U NU in 1962, the then Prime Minister, the nation was thrown into violence for decades to come. The brutal military regime crushed student protests and any and every resistance to its legitimacy.

And in a tiny village of Namsang in the Shan States of Burma, hours bus ride away from her hometown of Taunggyi, Jeeti, my cousin, slept for months with a ghost.

"Ko Hla yei, Ko Ko, why are you so wet and cold?"

Whenever Jeeti asked Ko Hla that question, he would get up from their rattan bed, lift the white mosquito netting and disappear into the cold rainy night and mist of the village, so she stopped asking him.

With the rising mist came the memory and ache in her heart of the blindfolded Ko Hla, a member of the Village Militia, protecting them from the violence of the Shan Independence Soldiers and the Burmese Tamadaw army, shot six times, first in his ankles, then his knees, his chest and head by a Burmese Tatmadaw soldier within hearing distance in their neighbor's hut where he was summoned for a meeting.

For three years afterwards, the dead Ko Hla kept her company.

She held him tight every night and made sure he was warm. She gave him sniff kisses. Months passed and she remained cocooned in his love and warmth.

No more rainy nights and cold days.

One day, as the sun rose over the banyan tree in the village square, the crows cawing, the sparrow tittering, Jeeti, who listlessly picked tiny bits of stones from the broken rice kernels, looked up as the fog lifted, seeing their beautiful daughters, Win Win and Ma Tin, as if without the gossamer veil of memory, and saw the naked yearning in their eyes.

That evening, after her duty at the village clinic ended where she was a nurse, Jeeti sat with her daughters and the other Pa'O and Shan women from around the village. They sat under the banyan tree, where the local ghosts dwell, and taught them how to knit and crochet. If one thread is weak or broken, the other holds the fabric up, she thought. *Look at this beautiful pattern, made up of all kinds of threads. Raw and polished.*

Years later, the son she thought she had lost forever came back to live with her. Mon To: her first-born, a sacrifice, and an offering. He was the one she left behind in Taunggyi with her forbidding Sikh father who had disowned her for marrying a Danu Shan man. When he returned, he simply said, "Ahmai, I am home."

Yes, with the rising mist, her heart, which ached for Ko Hla, found solace, bit by bit, in teaching Mon To, Win Win and Ma Tin the history of the Danu people and of the brave Danu Prince, an archer, who, legend had it, saved seven princesses trapped in the Pindiya Cave near Taunggyi by a human-sized spider through the use of his bow, the *dhanu*.

"You come from a brave people, who use the bow and arrow for the freedom of those trapped by injustice. Bow your head only in respect, but never in fear. Lift a weapon for the freedom of the oppressed and suffering."

A year later, Mon To and Win Win, we learned, joined the people's resistance army and have not been heard from in years.

Red Henna: Color Me

Red: The color of blood. The color of passion. The color of sunsets. The color of Indian bridal clothes. The red dupatta. The red chunni. The fabric draped over the Gurugranth Sahib, red. Red wine. Wounds. Lips. Cheeks. Cherries. Roses. When I was to become a bride, I, along with my mother Tej and sister Rina, went to Chandni Chowk to buy my bridal clothes and we came upon a red and gold *duppata*, a gauzy scarf, that we bought to go with my red silk salwar kameez, which my mother had sewn. My mamajis, my mother's brothers, were going to give me fake ivory churas bangles painted red to go with my bridal clothes. I had red lipstick and red *bindi* with red dots around my eyes. I was 25 years old and wore a red sweater knitted by my mother—on a bitterly cold winter day in January. We sat under an outdoor tent, a shamiana, which was red and white for the religious wedding ceremony, and the bitter winds blew.

Red: The color of the fabric Laaj, my grandmother, wove and dyed in Punjab. She used colors of red and fuchsia to embroider the phulkari cloth. All brides made phulkari with their friends before the wedding to bring to their in-law's house as dowry. The fabric she carried to Burma when she married my grandfather in Punjab during the British Raj. The fabric she carried back to Punjab when she fled Burma during the Japanese war. The one she used as a shawl when they had to flee in the middle of the night as refugees of the Partition back to Burma. She brought it back to India when she became a refugee after three decades in Burma due to the military cop. The fabric we cut up into little pieces and used as covers for our poorly made tables and furniture in our small, rented apartment in New Delhi. She gave me the last piece of the *phulkari* at my wedding.

Red: The color of henna on my hands and feet on my wedding day. We sat on the sun-warmed flat roof. The henna woman came and decorated my fingers, palms, wrists, arch of my ankles and part of the calves. If the color was really red, the Muslim henna artist told me, your in-laws would love you deeply. The color was dark red. They didn't.

Red Henna Blues

Three days after your arranged marriage, your new husband, seemingly in a kind manner, holding your hand at a posh Delhi café in Connaught Place, says, *our marriage will work only one way—it has to be 100% my way or 100% your way; it cannot be 50/50.* Confusion fighting with panic, you gaze questioningly at his bearded and turbaned face a kind face, really, rounded cheeks, eyes large and brown fringed by dark thick lashes, a few years older than you, but a serious face, so different from your own playful and constantly smiling one. He looks at your face, small, thin, your long thick hair tied up at the nape of your neck and pats your hands, the hands of a newlywed that are still hennafresh red and adorned with red and gold glass bangles, along with a set of fake ivory ones from your uncles.

You came to the café directly from your older brother's wedding ceremony where, as the sister of the groom, you had wholeheartedly celebrated, singing, dancing, mingling, and talking animatedly with all your brother's friends and guests. At the festivities, you had looked at your new husband sitting by your father's side, somber, still a stranger, one who touched you on your wedding night three days ago for the first time, briefly, but stopped when you became breathless. He looked at you, his expression inscrutable. Did he like what he saw in your bright indigo blue tissue silk sari with the big red bindi in the middle of your forehead and your red henna decorated hands with the long red nails? But immediately after lunch, he asked to talk to you, so there you were, sitting with a curious heart, the tea getting lukewarm and your favorite chicken pakora going cold in the plate. The old-fashioned jazz group dressed in red jackets and black trousers played Nat King Cole's "When Autumn Leaves."

When he said you would have to either go his way or yours, you knew if you said yours, you would probably be sent home in disgrace to your parents, immigrants from Burma, struggling to feed and educate you and your siblings in the crazy city of Delhi, so you lowered your kohl-rimmed eyes, unclasped your cold hands from his, took a sip of the now cold tea. He said, again, not too unkindly, *if you want it to be your way, I will go with it. Then, you will really have to lead and manage everything.* Why did you hear a threat in his voice? You had hoped for kindness, affection, babies and perhaps contentment and the ability to add your voice to some family decisions. After all, you were an educated and liberated woman from New Delhi now, weren't you? But, you imagined it had to be his way as you were leaving your natal family, going to live with him in an unfamiliar state, no job, no friends. You lifted your chin and titled your head. He must have noted the imperceptible tilt of your head as acquiescence. For he smiled, his full lips half hidden by his dark mustache: *I'm glad you understand. I'm doing this for your own good. You will now be a wife. You will have to interact with other officers and their wives at the factory. I want you to be dignified. As it is, your laugh is too loud, you open your mouth too wide, you speak too animatedly and hurriedly, and you walk too fast. All this must stop. Speak softly and rarely. Laugh in modicum and gently. Walk with grace and slowly.*

As his voice floated slowly over the sad jazz music, you zoned out for about 20 years, only occasionally making an appearance as the original you: even when your body, which was initially touched with hesitation and reverence, became deadened due to scorn, even when you occasionally exploded in pain and disappeared from home to walk for hours in the rain, even when your children saw fear in your eyes and you saw it reflected in theirs, even when you went back to school and read about violence and resistance in texts.

You remained submerged in the promise until you returned to you, for you lifted your eyes and could see beyond the veil and recognized that the sky is blue, after all, and the dancing waves of the pacific matched your own exuberant steps, leading you to yourself and your voice which you yourself have created for yourself and for others who came after you and accepted the power of belief in self and in love, a true love beyond conditions, beyond censure, beyond dualities—you returned to yourself as a pelican, gliding in the warm spring breeze, and skimmed the surface of the blue ocean for miles upon miles in meditative concentration and hope, swooping to the cool water's depth to snatch a fish, flying to the blue sky to swallow it, for sustenance, for growth, for nutrition, for ecological balance and the balance of karma and dharma, or to smash and break them for reconstruction, regeneration and regrowth.

The Diasporic Search for Home

The snow is like crushed white pearls and diamonds. It's powdered to a glittering sheen on the surface of the earth. Lake Superior is covered with a frozen shawl, a shining sheet of ice. The beach is covered in snow and mixed with grains of sand. Half formed waves frozen midair. The air cuts through the trees, whipping my hair into my mouth. I know I'm in love with the Upper Peninsula of Michigan, the UP, in the city of Marquette: When I see dogs yipping and running through the crowd of cheering family members for the sled dog races, little children in full snow suits, sitting on shoulder of fathers and mothers; when I see sparkling pure and white new snow, as I weave my way in my long waxed skis in the blueberry ridge ski trails; the mere thought of leaving the UP makes my heart sink and I fondly and fascinatingly gaze at the frozen lake and the snow for hours until, yes, until the dark days and the wet snow and the harsh cruel winds that find their way through the small cracks in my small old Victorian home—through the cracks in the floor and through the cracks in the walls and through a faulty heating systems and through the shoes that I wear and through warm brown new fur and leather boots and through the silk thermal underwear and long johns and through the UP Stormy Cromer I pull way down to my ears, through the thick warm scarf that mother had knitted for me years ago, and through my dreams and nightmares, through my waking days and nights, and through my hands and feet, and through my painful bones and fingers.

Then I think I'm delusional when I see signs of spring and the frozen earth cracking, little flowers peak their heads from the snow and the lake begins to melt and warm slow winds blow. And I smile and think:

I can't wait to slowly swim in the blue lake.
I can't wait to crunch the new snow as I cross-country ski.

I know I will soon forget the abusive cold.
and torturous days nights:

my home, where are you?

IV. Full Circle and Back

Burma Coups: 1962 & 2021

Inciting "hatred and contempt" towards the Myanmar military coup leaders can land you in prison for 20 years. If one were to incite anger towards the military Junta, "by words, either spoken or written, or by signs, or by visible representation," one could be detained by the Junta indefinitely without a trial. Protesters are surrounded by eight-wheeled armored military vehicles on the streets of Yangon, Mandalay, Myitkyina. Rubber bullets and bricks fly day and night. Aung San Suu Kyi is detained. No court hearing or ruling are needed for arrests. This is 2021.

I lived through the coup of 1962. Our home was periodically ransacked by the Burma Bureau of Special Investigations. After my father's shop was nationalized, rifles pointed at my father and mother's faces. Our cupboards searched for smuggled goods. My mother's clothes and makeup, a new Pond's talcum powder box, opened and strewed in the bedroom. My underwear and bra scattered on the bed. On 7 July 1962, my sister, Bubbly, who was in medical school in Rangoon, faced the violence of the army when the students protest movement was crushed and when scores of students were killed, hundreds of bodies buried in shallow graves, while others disappeared.

Dangerous Sun

Streets filled with demonstrators, once again, as it did decades ago when the military seized power and overturned a democratically elected Burmese government.

That was 1962.
This is 2021.

i learned to wear Burmese clothes, blue *longyi* and white *inji*, to the nationalized Convent School, as my white tunic and white longsleeved shirt, uniforms of our schools, was replaced by the government due to nationalism & our teachers and nuns exiled to other countries.

my cousin became a drug addict and died in his teens. My nephew, at age sixteen, unable to see his mother's hunger drove a borrowed truck to China's border and brought contraband goods. He was apprehended and imprisoned for decades; addicted to drugs, he died at a young age. my neighbor's sons died of drug addiction and their parents perished in poverty and heartache.

father's shop, nationalized, became the People's Shop. Jobless, he turned to the night market to hustle for a few kyats, selling mother's meagre jewelry to feed the family, buying fake watches from Kengtung.

daily, i was indoctrinated
        at morning school assembly
                to walk the Burmese way
                        to socialism path, to forget
                                democracy, freedom, free speech

but i, not yet twelve, saw father
and brother hide from the
Bureau of Special Investigations
nightly & remembered for decades

        I never forgot the dangerous *Sun*.

Nine Days After the Military Coup in Burma: 9 February 2021

two days before her birthday, Mya Thwet Thwet Khine, who shared a birthday with my four-year-old granddaughter, was shot dead in Naypyitaw, the shadow capital city of Burma:

only nineteen years old, she was protesting the military coup & when the security police shot at them with water cannons, she hid from the shooters.

but a bullet, marked with the bloody hands of the perpetrators—
found her long dark hair

      & penetrated her helmet . . .

Tantric Dancer

Crooked teeth, crinkled hair, eons ago, or so it seems, you smiled. Crouch in the bushes, hush, you call. Creeping around in the dark house, so as not to wake anyone. Body crushed, probed, torn, lies there in the dark, eyes glued shut. Breasts tender and sore, limbs tired and bruised; in the dark night, dreaming of a soothing presence.

Not demonized? Is there such a place? The door is open.

Crawling in, all wet from the ocean; why are you so cold? Turning grotesque humor into eunuch dances, into performance of Madams at whore houses of India, Mausi, for your judgmental community, so interesting, how you, Pu Lia, can enact parody so well. Drums beat at Christmas gathering, at his house, the house that is loved by all, so upper class, so Victorian. Out of place, alienated, you become bawdy. Or become a domestic goddess. They say, fuck her to subdue her. *"Aurat ko chahiyei na taaj na thakaht, usko chaiyei ek lund sakhat."* *Women need neither crown nor kingdom; all she needs is a hard dick.*

She is now here, now lost. Chameleon eyes detect her. Delicate dance, but aggressive moves. Realms unknown, unseen, meditative but also swirling energies. Kill her in the dark; rebirth also in dark shadows. Amalgamated in hybrid spaces.

Jumped out of the second-floor window and climbed down the Douglas Fir tree in the middle of the moonlit night—soared away, far away to the Atlantic Ocean and waded deep into the water; woke up refreshed.

And voices call. Come! Come! So sure, so resolute, so aware . . .

5. Historical Photos of the Singh and the Extended Family

Fig. 35: Daya Kaur, Tej Kaur's elder sister at the age of 14; she died a year later after giving birth to a stillborn daughter, circa 1930 in Taunggyi

Fig. 36: Laaj's brother, great-paternal uncle, Arjun Das, in Mongnai, Shan States, circa 1958

Fig. 37: Tej Kaur's youngest brother, Yuvaraj Singh aka Kaka with his new bride, Gurmat Kaur of Amritsar, Punjab, circa 1955

Fig. 38: Prab Joth Singh, sitting on the extreme right of the frame with his Taunggyi Tennis Club group, circa 1959

Fig. 39: Kuldip, Satya, and Jaspal, in Syrism (Thanlyin), circa 1958

Bibliography

Hal. "About Monk Isai: Founder of Tea." 23 Feb. 2008, www.ikedokitea.com/2020/10/01/about-monk-eisaifounder-of-japanese-tea/. Accessed 11 Feb. 2020.

Popsescu, Andra. "Origins and Myths of Tea." 20 April 2023, www.saichodrinks.com/blogs/news/origins-and-myths-of-tea. Accessed 9 Mar. 2020.

"The Origins of Tea: The Origins of Shenong and the Divine Leaf." www.theenlightenmentjourney.com/the-origin-of-tea-legend-of-shennong-and-the-divine-leaf/#. Accessed 9 Mar. 2020.

Walia, Pushpinder. "A Forgotten Utopia." *India Today.* www.indiatoday.in/magazine/supplement/story/20080303-a-forgotten-utopia-735533-2008-02-22. Accessed 20 May 2023

Acknowledgments

I would like to thank Patricia Killelea, my soul sister, for selflessly sharing her creative energy with me through the years. To Matthew Gavin Frank, my fellow traveler, for continuing to inspire me with his love for words and his zest for life.

Thank you, Northern Michigan University, Cape Peninsula University of Technology and University of the Western Cape, and to the students and cohorts, who walked with me during my diasporic journey; to my friends in Michigan, in South Africa, in India, and in the UK, to my family in the diaspora, who trusted me to share their stories and memories and to allow me to share mine during late night chai sessions in freezing snowy climes, or drinking copious amounts of *nimbu sharbat*s in the tropical heat, or being hedonistic with too much *laphet tot* and fried garlic chili salads with red wine by the largest lake on earth—you travelled with me, so thank you!

I extend gratitude to Uzma Ahmad for the cover painting of the photograph of the author; to Prithvipal Singh for clicking the photo and to Jane Milke for the digital image of the phulkari shawl. And to the late U Chan of Taunggyi who clicked many of the photos of my family in Burma.

To my children, Gautam and Gitanjali Singh, who, through tormenting times, stood by me. To my granddaughter, Karina Cho, with her ever-sparkling eyes and a ready laugh, for inspiring me to leave a legacy of words.

Appreciation goes to the publishers and to editors of journals where some essays first appeared: "Interconnected: You and I" and "You and I: Interconnected Beyond the Mountains" by Finishing Line Press; "Hullaballoo in Taunggyi" *in Branching Out: International Tales of Brilliant Flash Fiction "bakri, the badluck daughter" by Weber—The Contemporary West;* "Reading Byron in Burma" first appeared in another version as "Shades of Love: English Toffee" in *The Offbeat: With Abandon.*

The photographs from my childhood were taken by my late family members.

www.ingramcontent.com/pod-product-compliance
Lightning Source LLC
Chambersburg PA
CBHW020237030726
47497CB00009B/3142